A PILLAR OF THE COMMUNITY

EUSTACE PALMER
(Doc P.)

Sierra Leonean Writers Series
(CW-15)

A Pillar of the Community

ISBN: 978-9988-1-47525

Sierra Leonean Writers Series
c/o Mallam O. & J. Enterprises
120 Kissy Road, Freetown, Sierra Leone
Publisher: Osman Sankoh (Mallam O.)
publisher@sl-writers-series.org /

Dedicated to the memory of my late
brothers:

Frederick, Prince, and Cecil;

and to the only

surviving one:

Stanley

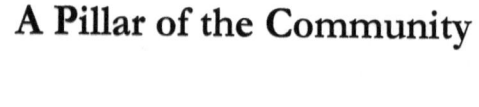

A Pillar of the Community

CHAPTER 1

Jedidiah Thomas, B.Sc. O.R. had become a pillar of the community. He had to be. How could an Officer of the Most Excellent Order of the Rokel not be a pillar of the community? An honor such as that was only given to those who had distinguished themselves in their chosen professions or in public life: individuals who had risen to the top by sheer hard work and perseverance, or who had been so single-minded in pursuit of the task in hand that their exemplary conduct had been brought to the attention of the President of the Republic. He thus singled them out for national recognition, honor and praise. Had not the President himself, His Excellency, Commander in Chief of the Armed Forces and Fountain of Honor, pinned the insignia of the award on his breast and shaken his hand in a grip so vice-like and intimate that it signified his welcome to that select group, the pillars of the community? Scoffers might say that such honors were cheap; that favoritism and nepotism played a much more important role in the selection of the recipients than excellence, merit and competence; that one was much more likely to be honored in this way if one had devoted one's life to licking the bottom or shoes of some important personage. Let them scoff, Jedidiah would say to himself. They only said those things because they were eaten up with jealousy and envy --failures, all of them, whose names would never feature in the distinguished list of recipients of national awards. He, Jedidiah Thomas, knew that he richly deserved his recognition and honor.

Even if he had not been a pillar of the community before receiving this award, the award itself automatically made him one of the elect. Had his name not been broadcast on the national radio throughout New Year's Day as the list of recipients was read out? Had he not received congratulatory messages, letters, and phone calls? Had not many people he met in the street, at church or at work saluted him and told him that he had proved himself a most distinguished son of the soil and that everyone was proud of him? Had not even his enemies in the civil service kowtowed to him with the utmost sycophancy, completely forgetting that he was the cause of their being denied a promotion, a scholarship, government quarters or a loan? Had he not been invited to the glorious investiture ceremony at State House itself? Was he not being invited by all sorts of organizations to be Distinguished Grand Chief Patron, or Distinguished Grand Chief Worshipper? Had his stock not risen among his fellow freemasons, and was he not in line for succession to the Master's position? Had not the honor done to him boosted his campaign during the church elections and secured him an easy victory as People's Warden over a wealthier and more pompous opponent?

Yes! There was no doubt about it. He was now truly a pillar of the community, one of the people who really mattered, and he was determined to retain this position come hell or whatever. He had struggled all his life to achieve this kind of position and recognition and no one, but no one, was going to take it away from him. If anyone dared to say or do anything that might jeopardize his position, he would skin him alive! He would make him regret the day he was born! He, Jedidiah Thomas, B.Sc., OR, People's Warden, Master-to-be, Permanent Secretary, would never let that happen to him.

One fine late afternoon in June, clad only in a pair of khaki shorts and a white singlet, his six foot frame stretched out on a hammock, Jedidiah Thomas was relaxing on the balcony of his five-year-old mansion on Juba Hill, overlooking the sea. The house had been appropriately named, 'My Repose.' As he enjoyed the beauty of the waves lashing the shore, and the three-mile-long beach where he could see footballers playing, fishermen and fisherwomen haggling over the price of newly landed fish, and hosts of near naked tourists enjoying the warmth of the tropical sun, thousands of miles away from their own snow-covered lands, Jedidiah stretched an arm towards the bottle of Heineken beer that stood on a stool near him. He took a deep swig from it, sighed with contentment, and replaced it on the stool. Life was good! Yes! Even in this poverty-stricken land where street children roamed around and scrounged from dustbins in competition with the dogs, where scores died unnecessarily every day from malnutrition or lack of proper medical attention, where even a fairly well dressed person who approached you was as likely as not to be a beggar, life was good. He had made it, and he was enjoying the fruits of his labor.

Jedidiah Thomas, or Jedi as his mother called him, and as he came to be known to those closest to him, was forty-nine and had good reason to believe that he would live for at least another thirty years. He enjoyed robust health, a fact he attributed not just to his rather austere and abstemious life, but to his indulging in rigorous exercise every morning, and also to the mixture of raw egg and orange juice which he swallowed even before taking his bath. It was this rigorous regime that ensured that, while most of his contemporaries had grown potbellies that hung over their belts like burdensome bags of rice, he still retained the figure of a young man. His abdominal muscles were hard and very firm. His biceps bulged like a middleweight boxer's. His chest looked like a lion's, and his thighs and legs were as strong as those of an ox. His jet-black skin seemed to ooze health from every pore, and shone as though it had been polished with shea butter. Not a single strand of gray was visible in his abundant hair; not one of his teeth was missing; and only one scar on his right leg, the relic of a minor accident while he was a boy, marred the supple smoothness of his skin. Indeed, Jedidiah Thomas could easily have passed for thirty-four, a fact which he used to advantage in those situations when he wanted to pass for a young man.

Jedi took another swig from the bottle of Heineken, sighed deeply, belched loudly, and half closed his eyes as the cool early evening breeze from the Atlantic fanned him lightly. With his arms, thighs, legs and broad chest exposed to the breeze's caressing ministrations, he felt a tingling sensation all over his body. Yes! Life was good.

It was inevitable that in this euphoric mood Jedi should start having vaguely erotic fantasies. His eyes still half shut, he smiled as he remembered the scores of girls and young women who had been at his beck and call over the years. He thought of the ease with which he had seduced them and taken them to his bed and made them squeal and squirm with pleasurable pain, made them feel the weight and power of those boxer's arms and wrestler's body and thighs, made them scream out his name in ecstasy and beg him to "kill" them. Yes! Life was good.

Gradually, Jedi started to doze; then one of those involuntary jerks that sometimes accompany the process of falling asleep, almost upset the unfinished bottle of Heineken. He awoke with a start; only just in time to stop the bottle from crashing on to the tiled floor of the balcony. As he set the bottle to rights, he turned his head slightly and his eyes landed on the most terrifying sight he had seen in his entire life. His heart missed ten beats and sweat broke out on his forehead in spite of that cooling breeze which had been fanning it so seductively only a few moments earlier.

What Jedi saw with such consternation was nothing more nor less than a girl in school uniform, walking up the street towards his house. Now the sight of a young girl primly dressed in her school uniform should not normally cause consternation; certainly not to an innocent mind, especially as the girl herself, dressed so neatly and decently, looked the very picture of innocence. Why should her sudden appearance throw the principled pillar of the community into such a state of terror? The fact was that in spite of being a pillar of the community with an undoubted reputation for sobriety and moral rectitude, Jedi, like so many other men of his status, had a secret vice. His weakness, up till then carefully concealed from the outside world, was an almost pathological fondness for seducing adolescent girls.

He had never married, a fact that he attributed to his determination to throw all his energy into his career and climb steadily up the ladder of preferment. At least, this was how he justified his prolonged bachelorhood to his relations, and to acquaintances who cared to ask. That is, until he admitted to himself that the real reason was his attraction to girls of, sixteen, seventeen or so. Any woman over the age of eighteen left him absolutely cold. Oh, he had had relationships with older women, several of them, scores of them, but it had been just animal pleasure. They had all left him absolutely cold. Now, if it had been possible for him to marry a girl of sixteen or seventeen.... It was true that in the past, and even now among certain African tribes, middle-aged men married girls of sixteen, but how could he, in this modern age and given his ethnic background, marry a teenager? That did not happen among his own people. And, in any case, girls of sixteen were in the habit of growing up. What would he do when his sweet teenager turned twenty or twenty-one?

Once Jedi diagnosed his condition, he had taken his mind back to his youth and early manhood for its first signs and symptoms, and realized that they had always been there and could have been recognized if anyone, including himself, had bothered to look for them. When he was fourteen, fifteen and sixteen, it had been perfectly natural for him to have girl friends of fourteen, fifteen and sixteen, but even when he turned seventeen, eighteen and nineteen, even twenty, he had continued to prefer girl friends in their early teens. His friends teased him now and then about his going with "babies," but it was not seriously meant, because boys of their age often had girl friends who were three years or so younger. No one had considered his preference as being in any way abnormal, and neither had he, until, as a young teacher of twenty-one or twenty-two, he discovered that he could not take his eyes off some of the fifteen and sixteen-year-old girls in the third and fourth forms of the school where he taught English and mathematics as a young graduate. He kept fantasizing about them and seized every opportunity to put his arms around their shoulders and tease them. Some of the girls evidently had crushes on him; after all, he was the youngest and most attractive of the male teachers. Some of the girls even contrived to visit him at home on the pretext of going for private lessons. Jedi could easily have taken advantage of his position and seduced them, but, in those days, he had high principles and had decided that fooling around with his pupils was wrong and unprofessional. Besides, he knew that he would never live down the shame and disgrace if the parents discovered such an affair. In any case, he had no opportunity to seduce girls at home because he still lived with his mother in those days. She was determined that Jedi should not become like the father who had abandoned them for another woman, and she had taught her son to follow the paths of righteousness. To keep Jedi on the straight and narrow, she always contrived to be around whenever the girls came for their 'lessons'.

So Jedi had contented himself with merely flirting and indulging in his fantasies until the day he decided that if he continued to restrain what he considered to be his real nature, he would slowly burn up inside. He then began to yield to his secret desire as discreetly as he could; but as he grew older, he realized that seducing young girls had become an obsession. He spent most Saturday and Sunday afternoons at the juvenile discos known irreverently as 'Sunday Schools', where the dancing was intended for teenagers, but it was perfectly permissible for older men to sit at the bar enjoying, not only their drinks, but also the tantalizing sight of nubile young things prancing around singly, in groups or with their boyfriends; gyrating their hips and supple waists, while their ripe breasts trembled beneath thin blouses. It was at one such 'Sunday School' that Jedi met girl who was now walking towards his house in her school uniform.

On that day, he had just taken a sip of his Heineken when he noticed a petite girl coming through the lounge. He almost dropped his glass. The girl was hand in hand with an exceptionally tall young man whom Jedi took to be her boyfriend. *What a face!* he thought, staring. It was the most beautiful face he had ever seen, and he had seen many, with his favorite chocolate brown, complexion glowing like warm butter. She smiled at her boyfriend, and two glorious dimples appeared in her cheeks, making her look even younger than what he was sure was her age: sixteen. She radiated happiness and had an air of innocence that Jedi felt sure was quite deceptive; no boyfriend would allow such a captivating specimen of a girl to remain innocent for long. She had on a fawn-colored chiffon dress which barely reached her knees and exposed a good deal of her thighs and all of her long, elegant legs. She was wearing dark underwear under the dress, but he could still make out the molding of her hips and breasts.

The girl noticed Jedi's gaping mouth and popping eyes, understood what it meant and stared boldly back at him with the most delicious smile he had seen in years, before sauntering past him with her boyfriend.

Angels in Heaven! thought Jedi, W*hat a babe!. I just have to have her*!

And he wasted no time. He rose from his seat with his beer in one hand and went outside to take a vantage point on the edge of the courtyard. From there he could see the girl clearly as she danced with her boyfriend. Jedi made sure that she was never out of his sight and feasted his eyes on that lovely form, while his heart palpitated with growing lust. The girl continued to throw smiles and glances in his direction, and when she was sure that his eyes were riveted on her, wiggled her shapely hips even more provocatively. Without saying a word, Jedi had let her know that he wanted her; and she was dancing her consent. Had he not been consumed with lust, he might have thought her behavior quite shameless. However, a man in the throes of desire never criticizes the conduct of its object, especially when such conduct is an indication that she is equally attracted to him. This girl clearly knew what she was about and Jedi found himself saying almost audibly,

Yes! I am going to have her!

The rest was quite simple. There was usually a scramble for transport at the end of the 'Sunday school'. That was the best time for pouncing on the prey, so as soon as Jedi realized that the girl and her boyfriend were leaving, he started moving towards the car park. The girl had thrown him an even more meaningful look, which seemed to say, "If you really want me, make your move now or lose me, perhaps forever." Jedi understood that look. He got his car out and drove slowly until he was nearly abreast of the young couple. The girl turned round and smiled. Her boyfriend also turned round, and put out his hand to signify that they were looking for a ride. Much later, it occurred to Jedi that it was a matter of supreme irony that it was in fact the boyfriend who had asked him for a ride and thus facilitated the seduction of his girlfriend. It was considered a matter of honor for a boyfriend to secure a ride for his girlfriend; it boosted his masculine ego. Little did the boyfriend know that in the act of satisfying his male ego, he was sending his girl into the arms of a middle-aged man.

During the drive, Jedi skillfully drew out personal information from the girl and, to avoid suspicion, from her boyfriend, and communicated as much about himself as he thought necessary for his purpose. He found out that her name was Emma King and that she was in the third form at school. He found out where she lived, where she went to school, and what she did with her spare time. He also told her where he worked, what his position was and where he lived. He asked the young man a few questions, but could barely remember his name, let alone what he said he did for a living. Jedi knew that he and the girl were playing a game, and what made it all the more enjoyable was that the boyfriend seemed quite unaware of their motives and intentions. He had no doubt that the girl would look him up afterwards

And she did; but what Jedi did not expect was that she would come to his office and in broad daylight. He had just finished dictating a letter to his secretary one afternoon, when the female typist buzzed to tell him that there was a young lady, as she put it, in the outer office to see him.

"Let her come in, Mrs. Cole," he told his secretary as she left the office, and soon afterwards, there was a light tap on the door.

"Come right in," he called out, then almost jumped out of his seat as a young girl in a blue and white school uniform tripped into the room. It took him a few moments to realize that it was Emma King, for in her school uniform she looked even younger than her sixteen years.

Jedi did not associate Emma King with innocence, yet there she was in front of him the very picture of that quality.

But this was not what made him almost jump out of his seat. It was common knowledge that some middle-aged men in the civil service were having liaisons with juveniles, "juvies," as they were called. Most of these 'sugar daddies' did their best to keep these affairs secret, so the worst thing that could happen to them was for a juvenile lover to turn up at the office in her school uniform. It meant she had just come from school. The whole office then surmised that she had come to engage in some shady activity with their boss before going home.

Jedi felt even more embarrassed because, in her uniform, Emma King could really have passed for fifteen or even fourteen. What would Mrs. Cole say? What would the clerks and typists and messengers say? Would they spread the rumor that their own Mr. Thomas, whom they had always believed to be a model of integrity, sobriety, and continence, was having an affair with a schoolgirl? Oh my God! He would never be able to live down the disgrace. He would never be able to maintain discipline in that office after that. And Mrs. Cole had just respectfully and thankfully obtained his consent to serve as Distinguished Grand Chief Patron at the annual thanksgiving service of her Mothers' Union. He was quite sure that she had asked him, not just because she knew he would make a substantial donation, but because she considered him a worthy and exemplary pillar of the community. Now this!

Emma was completely taken aback to see Mr. Thomas's chagrined expression and the beads of sweat that had formed on his temple. Her face fell and her knees went suddenly weak. What was the matter? Could it be that Mr. Thomas was having second thoughts? That he no longer wanted her? Had she come all this way and braved going through that office full of gossiping clerks, secretaries and messengers to be rebuffed like this? A minute later, she realized the source of the trouble.

"Shut the door, please," Jedi said, sounding official, then went on in a hushed and agitated voice:

"Why have you come here in your school uniform? Don't you know that you will cause all kinds of rumors about us? Why did you have to visit me in my office? Couldn't you have gone to my house in the evening?"

So that was all, thought Emma as she flashed her beautiful smile and took the seat that Jedi had not offered her. Oh these men! They were all the same! Always wanting their fun, but unwilling to be found out.

"But Mr. Thomas, you talked so much about your work and your office that I thought you wanted me to come here," she lied. "If I had known that you wanted me to go to your house, I would have gone to your house. In any case, you did not mention your wife..."

It was true that Jedi had not told Emma and her boyfriend that he was a bachelor. It had simply not occurred to him at the time.

"Did I tell you that I had a wife?" He muttered, a note of lingering irritation in his voice. "You will find no one in my house when you visit me. I have no wife. There is only my houseboy, and he is usually off work at about five when I return from work. There will be no one to disturb us, my dear. We shall be absolutely alone, just the two of us."

Jedi's tone, which up to this point had been a little rough due to his anxiety and annoyance, softened noticeably as he said those last words. He now leaned over his desk and lovingly covered Emma's dainty hand with his. The anxiety had been caused by her stupidity in coming to his office in her school uniform, but the irritation was at least partly caused by the fact that he had felt slightly cheated. He had wanted Emma to visit him at home where he could have her all to himself and they would not have to hide from prying eyes and idle gossips. For one chagrined moment he had felt that the girl had decided to play hard to get or perhaps did not intend to capitulate after all, in spite of the signals she had sent to him at the 'Sunday School'. Now, however, her statement about a possible wife reassured him. He knew that she was more than willing to yield to his advances.

As if to reassure him further, in response to the pressure from his large strong hand, Emma increased hers gradually, lowered her eyelids, and gently tickled the inside of his palm with her index finger. Her half-closed eyes gazed straight into his, and a little smile played around her soft lips. Jedi felt desire rise powerfully in him and his heart began to pound.

She is mine! She is mine! I will have her! he exulted silently. *Wow! She seems* so *knowing, so experienced! God! Innocent young girls don't exist any more.*

It never occurred to Jedidiah Thomas that he was one of the reasons there weren't any innocent young girls left in the city. He was about to ask Emma when she would visit him at home when she herself asked in a seductive murmur,

"Well, when do you want me to visit you at home, Mr. Thomas?"

They made the appointment in whispers, and at the end, Jedi warned her not to visit him at the office any more, unless it was unavoidable, and certainly not in her school uniform. Only after all this was settled did Jedi suddenly realize that he had to find some kind of explanation for those inquisitive office gossips, who, he was sure, were straining their ears in the ante-room, trying to hear some of his conversation with Emma. He now asked Emma in a loud voice how she was getting on at school and how her mother, Cousin Ayo, was doing. Emma immediately understood what he was up to and played her part to perfection. Her fertile imagination invented all kinds of difficulties that her mother was going through and sounded so convincing that Jedi was sure Mrs. Cole and her clique would believe her even if they did not believe him. There was genuine dismay and sympathy in Jedi's voice as he told Emma he was extremely sorry to hear that Cousin Ayo was ill, and that she should take back his good wishes to her; that he would make a point of visiting them after work on Friday with some provisions and financial help to tide them over. Emma thanked him with the utmost respect. Thus, Jedi killed two birds with one stone. He had made sure that Emma would visit him at home and he had, he hoped, stopped the tongues of Mrs. Cole's and her colleagues from wagging.

Emma had visited him at home, not only on the agreed date, but on several other occasions. The three months they had been together were among the happiest periods in Jedi's entire life for he was constantly amazed by Emma's resourcefulness as a lover. She seemed an inexhaustible store of new ideas to keep him aroused and fulfilled, carrying him on wave after wave of passion during which he seemed to lose his mind, regain sanity, lose it again, pounce and claw with the ferocity of a tiger, get a grip on himself and move with the elegance of a swimmer on softly billowing waters, swoon with delicious ecstasy, then bounce back to life and explode like a cannon ball Where on earth had the girl gained all that knowledge and experience at her age, he often wondered. Surely, not from that young lover of hers! Whoever said it was wrong to make love to young girls did not know a thing. This was the life! Let them ask him; he knew.

The affair had been going swimmingly when Jedi turned his head on the day in question and saw the delectable Emma approaching his house, dressed in her school uniform. She had never visited him at home in her school uniform before. What on earth had got into her? Hadn't he already told her not to visit him in her uniform? Well, he remembered that he had specifically said that she should not visit him in the office dressed in her uniform, but he assumed that an intelligent and worldly-wise girl like her would understand that the restriction applied to his home as well. Why was she acting so strangely? Was she doing it deliberately to throw him off balance or to assert her independence as she often did?

He knew that Emma would now be almost at the gate and that he should go downstairs and let her in quickly before she started attracting comment from the neighbors. He was about to jump out of the hammock, when it occurred to him that some neighbor might be watching him and that his jumping briskly out of the hammock might attract suspicion. For all he knew that busybody, Mama Sawyerr, Clarence Thorpe's fat idle mother-in-law next door, had already seen Emma standing at his gate and would be straining her short fat neck to find out what was going on.

So Jedi moved as slowly and unobtrusively as possible from the balcony. But once he got into his bedroom, through which he had to pass in order to get downstairs, he ran like a man who had just been told that his house was on fire. Although he was almost fainting with trepidation, he opened the gate as noiselessly as possible, let Emma in while putting his left hand to his lips to indicate that she should not say a word, then shut the gate again trying not to make a sound. As soon as they were within the house and out of earshot he railed:

"Why have you come here in your uniform? Haven't I told you before not to visit me in your school uniform?"

"But Mr. Jedi, you said I should not visit you in your office in my school uniform. You never said anything about your house."

"Well, it comes to the same thing. Surely, you have intelligence; you should be able to understand that. I don't want us to do anything that will arouse suspicion or expose us to scandal. After all, you are a schoolgirl; do you want your name to be circulated around the whole town?"

"All right Mr. Jedi, I will not do it again. I am supposed to be attending a sports meeting at the stadium, so I dressed as though I was going to it, but I came straight here instead. I had to see you today, and the sports gave me a good alibi. Mr. Jedi, please don't be annoyed with me."

She said the last few words with a little pout, her voice almost tearful.

"I am only a little bit annoyed with you," Jedi said, putting his arms around her and speaking in as tender a tone as he could manage. God! Whenever she spoke to him in that soft, pleading, half-crying tone, whether it was genuine or faked, he could not help himself. It made her sound so young and soft and vulnerable and feminine that he felt extra strong and protective and powerful and could hardly wait to have her again.

So they had a most magnificent time together. Afterwards, as she half dozed in his arms, Jedi gazed at her slim young body with worshipful adoration. God! Wasn't he lucky! To think that all that youth and beauty and sweetness belonged to him! That he could have it whenever he wanted! That he was still enjoying what his male contemporaries had stopped enjoying decades ago! That he could make her scream and sob and writhe, throw her limbs about in wild abandon, scratch and claw, bite and beg and shudder in a way in which, he was sure, that oaf, her boyfriend, could never make her. He was sure he couldn't; otherwise, why did she keep returning week after week, at least once a week? Although he was old enough to be the boyfriend's father, he had strength, power and experience on his side, He felt immensely grateful to the Almighty for allowing him to enjoy such youth and beauty. Yes! Life could not be better. He was at the peak of his happiness.

Emma's beautiful face looked even more radiant with the eyes half shut and her lips apart. She moaned softly like one waking up from sleep, stretched, cuddled into his arms and then, quite inexplicably, began to sob.

"My dear," he said, quite concerned, "what on earth is the matter?"

Instead of answering, she cried even more vehemently. Jedi had to hold her tightly as her slender little body shook with sobs.

"Whatever it is," Jedi said, "please tell me. Let us solve the problem together. I am here to help you. Is your boyfriend giving you problems? If he is, tell me, and I'll deal with the clown. I know your father is dead, but I am here to take his place. I will deal with any boy who gives you problems. You just say the word."

But Emma exploded into even more heart-wrenching sobs. Jedi was quite perplexed.

"Emma, please tell me. Whatever it is, tell me. I am sure we can solve it between the two of us. You are not doing yourself any good by crying. Besides, some of the neighbors might hear you crying; and that will not do any good to my reputation. Come on! Stop this silliness and talk to me."

Emma seemed to decide that it was time to talk because she wiped her eyes with the back of her hand and said,

"Mr. Jedi, I have something to tell you. That is why I came today."

"Well, what is it?" Jedi snapped, anticipating some unwelcome information. "Has your boyfriend found out about us? Has your mother found out about us?"

"*What a foolish man!*" thought Emma. "*His only concern is that his filthy tricks should not be found out. He cannot think of anything more serious than that. Well, I'll let him have it straight. Let's see how he takes it.*"

"Mr. Jedi," she began, the tearfulness returning to her voice although her eyes were now quite dry. "Mr. Jedi, I couldn't find my period this month."

"What!" Jedi jumped up as though an electric current had passed through his body and towered over her. It was now Emma's turn to fear that he might alarm the neighbors. She began to feel that she should probably have broken the news more gently. Was he going to hit her? Her heart began to pound so fiercely that she felt breathless.

"What did you say?" Jedi shouted. His eyes looked wild and sweat had already appeared on his brow. "What did I hear you say?"

Emma was now crying in earnest.

"Oh my mother! Oh my mother! What shall I do? What shall I do?"

"I said what did I hear you say?" Jedi took her by the shoulders, half lifted her off the bed, and gave her a violent shake.

"I said ....I said I ...I did not see...my ...my ...my period this month, sir."

"Then you can bloody well go and find it wherever you left it," Jedi said coldly and let her fall back onto the bed.

His mind was in complete turmoil. He hadn't bargained for this. Well, he knew that if you had sex regularly with a full-grown female you should expect that she might sooner or later become pregnant. But somehow, Emma had seemed too young for that to happen. Too innocent. This was why he had hardly bothered to take the kind of precautions he might have taken with another woman. He simply could not associate pregnancy with her.

This was not the first time that a woman had told him that she was pregnant for him. He already had two children by two of those mature women whom he had been forced to go with for appearance's sake. They were grown women, and he had believed them as soon as they told him. But this girl! Just look at her lying down there crying her heart out! In any case, was she telling the truth? How could he be sure that she was telling the truth? Did he know her well enough to trust her?

"How do you know you are pregnant?" he asked pointlessly, and then added, "How do you know you are not mistaken?"

"Mr. Jedi, I know I am not mistaken. Apart from missing my period, I have been feeling dizzy and I have even vomited."

"Did you see a doctor?"

"Oh no, sir! I would be too ashamed. I only talked to my friends"

Well, that was something to be grateful for, Jedi thought. If she had seen a doctor, she could not have avoided dragging him into it. And how could he, a forty-nine-year-old senior civil servant admit to being responsible for a seventeen-year-old girl's pregnancy? No! It was good that she had not yet seen a doctor. Then something even more alarming occurred to him and he blurted out:

"Did you tell your friends that I am responsible?"

"Oh no, Mr. Jedi! I couldn't do that, sir. I had to talk to you first."

At this Jedi breathed a sigh of relief. At least, no one, apart from the two of them, knew about the father's identity. Not yet, anyway. But a nagging suspicion still troubled him. Could she be trying to place her pregnancy at his door in order to protect her worthless boyfriend who would certainly not have the means to do anything about it and was far from being ready for fatherhood? One could never trust these girls. They appeared as innocent as the day, but they could be as wily as the serpent himself, as wicked as Delilah. Perhaps Emma was trying to lay the pregnancy at his door to protect her worthless boyfriend. He could picture the scene: both of them laughing at him behind his back, calling him, 'Sugar daddy'! 'Juvie lover!' Yes! He could see it all now. What a fool he had been to think that she really cared for him and even preferred him to her boyfriend! How they must have laughed as they both squandered the money that he regularly gave her! He was their insurance policy, or more specifically, the boyfriend's insurance policy. That young savage must have known that he could plough Emma to his heart's content without fear of any consequences, since consequences would be laid at Mr. Jedi's door. What a fool he had been!

These confused thoughts so enraged Jedi that he took Emma roughly by the shoulders again.

"Even if you are pregnant, how do you know I am responsible?" he demanded, glaring down at her. "What about that boyfriend of yours? I am sure you have been messing around with him almost every day. If you think you can fool around with him and then lay the consequences at my door, you are very much mistaken. Go to him. I am sure you will find your period under his pillow."

As he said 'pillow', he pushed Emma back onto the bed. The girl was now sobbing pitifully.

"Oh God! Have mercy on me! What is going to happen to me? What is going to happen to me? If I had known that this was how you would react, I would never have let you touch me, Mr. Jedi. After I have allowed you to do whatever you like with me, after I have given myself to you freely, this is how you treat me! Like a dog! I do not blame you; I blame myself. I should have tried to be a good girl as my mother always warned me to be. It is more than two months since Abdul touched me. We quarreled, as I told you. It was because of you that I told him not to come near me anymore. I can swear on anything, drink anything to prove you are responsible. If I am lying, let the child inside me rot and kill me. Oh God! Oh my mother! I am finished! "

In spite of his utter self-absorption, Jedi was not a monster. He had genuine tender feelings towards Emma and the sight of her wailing so pitifully, softened his heart. Besides, the fact that she was prepared to swear a terrible oath convinced him that she was telling the truth and he was indeed the father of her child. How could he abandon a girl who had given him so much pleasure? Even if her boyfriend had been responsible, *he* had also eaten at that table. Surely all she would want from him was help with getting rid of the pregnancy. That wouldn't cost much; and he had the right contacts. Afterwards they could return to their sweet, cozy, relationship; just make sure they were more careful.

He sat down beside Emma to make amends for his harshness.

"Alright baby! I am sorry!" he cajoled. "I did not mean to hurt you. I do believe you and I will take care of everything. We will work it out, okay?...okay?. Come on! Stop crying...."

Emma was quite willing to be apologized to and comforted, for she had had horrible visions of being abandoned to her fate. She had already begun to see herself as a disgraced and ruined girl, forced to leave school, perhaps stigmatized for life. Inevitably, the change of atmosphere in Jedi's bedroom led to another bout of lovemaking, on this occasion, the most ecstatic that they had ever experienced. On the part of one it was inspired by gratitude and relief; on the part of the other by re-awakened lust and the recent confirmation of his potency. The pair seemed to go outside of themselves as they clawed at each other, reckless of any consequences. The tempo of their movements quickened fiercely as if they were being goaded by forces completely beyond their control. At the height of their passion Jedi roared like a lion pouncing upon a helpless victim. He grabbed Emma's slight body with all his strength as though afraid that she would escape from his grasp. As he triumphantly poured out his life-seed, he felt her shudder beneath him with uncontrollable spasms, as she let out the most deliciously satisfied sigh. Sated and exhausted himself, Jedi sank down on her with his whole weight and immediately fell into a deep sleep

They remained like that for quite a long time and it was Jedi who stirred first. He opened his eyes, looked at the clock by his bedside and realized that they must have slept for almost an hour, for it was already past seven o'clock. Darkness had set in. *My God!* he thought, rolling off Emma's motionless form. It was about time the girl was on her way. The sports meeting must be over and her mother would be expecting her back. Emma seemed to be in absolute repose, her face as radiant as an angel's. Jedi smiled fondly, congratulating himself for having brought about this look of heavenly contentment. Then he remembered that she was pregnant.

For a moment he could not believe that this innocent-looking little girl could possibly be pregnant. He kissed her lightly on the cheek then began the process of waking her up.

"Come on, baby!" he said, shaking her slightly, "it is time to wake up. It is time to go. Your mother will be getting anxious."

There was no response. Boy! He must have worn her out with his virility. He was feeling immensely proud of himself as he made a second attempt to rouse her.

"Emma, wake up! You really must wake up. It's already half past seven. It will probably be nine by the time you get home. Your mother will start asking questions. Wake up."

He shook her again, rather more strenuously this time, then realized something very odd. The girl had not even stirred. Indeed, her only movement had been caused by his shaking of her shoulders. What a naughty girl to be sleeping so soundly when her mother was probably getting frantic with worry! Another thing struck him as odd. Surely someone who was sleeping so soundly should be breathing heavily; that was the natural thing. Yet not a sound was coming from Emma. In fact, she did not seem to be breathing at all. A wave of alarm surged through Jedi's body and he jumped off the bed as though stung by a deadly snake. What on earth could have happened? Had the girl fainted? Or was she playing tricks with him? Taking Emma by the shoulders, he shook her once more, this time so roughly that the whole bed rattled as it never had before, not even at the height of their lovemaking.

"Stop playing these tricks Emma. Wake up! Wake up, or I'll slap you."

But the girl hung limp in his arms and the beautiful jaw now fell open. Beside himself with alarm and panic, Jedi put his ear to her nostrils. Not a sound! He then put his ear to her chest. Her heart was absolutely still. He felt her little palm. It was already quite cold.

CHAPTER 2

Jedi's jaw dropped. His eyes popped out like those of a captured rat that had just been dashed against a concrete floor. A cold sweat instantly covered his whole body as he began to contemplate the possibility that the girl might be dead. Dead? Surely not! Dead? In his bed! In his house! *Oh God! Let her not be dead! Please God, let her not be dead!* She couldn't be dead! Maybe she had only fainted; maybe she had only lost consciousness and would soon regain it. Maybe, if he shook her violently enough... At this he grabbed hold of Emma's shoulders once more and gave her the most violent shake of all.

"Come on, Emma! Wake up! Speak to me! Speak to me!" He sounded almost tearful as he continued his violent shaking of the small flaccid body. It was to no avail. Emma's body remained as limp and as lifeless as a piece of underwear that had been carelessly thrown into a laundry basket. It then occurred to Jedi that he might try artificial respiration. Maybe she was not yet dead, and if he tried mouth-to-mouth resuscitation, or massaged her heart, she could be revived. Jedi had no idea how to perform artificial respiration or mouth-to-mouth resuscitation, though he had seen them done in the movies. However, he was desperate enough to try anything.

He put his mouth close to Emma's, the way he had done countless times before to give her a passionate kiss. This time, doing that almost filled him with distaste. However, he persevered and blew great mouthfuls of air into her body, hoping it would somehow find its way into her lungs and revive her. He did it again and again and again, gradually increasing his tempo while at the same time massaging her heart, or where he thought her heart was. After about five minutes, he stopped and listened for a heartbeat, but there was still no sound. A tremendous panic now took hold of Jedi, but he still had a faint hope, and again threw himself into the heart massage and improvised artificial respiration with all his might and fury. This time he kept at it for a full fifteen minutes. But there was still no response, and he could feel the naked body under him growing colder and stiffer.

"Oh my God," he exclaimed in horror, "She can't be dead! Emma! What are you doing to me? You can't do this to me! You can't die in my bed and in my house! What are you doing to me?"

Jedi was now frantic and desperate, but he tried one last thing. He had heard that one could find out whether or not a person was dead by putting a clear mirror over the nostrils. If the mirror misted over, that meant that the person was breathing and therefore still alive. But if the mirror remained unclouded... Jedi could not bear to consider the alternative. He jumped out of the bed in all his nakedness, rushed to his chest of drawers, and took a small mirror out of the top drawer. Having polished it thoroughly with an edge of the white bed sheet, he pressed the mirror against Emma's nose, all the while silently willing her breath to cloud it.

"Come on! Come on!" he urged, not sure whom or what he was addressing: the lifeless girl, or the breath in her body.

"Come on! Come on!" he moaned, his despair increasing with each futile glance at the mirror. He continued holding it to Emma's nostrils for another thirty minutes, hoping against hope for a miracle; but nothing happened and, gradually, he allowed the fact to take possession of his consciousness, that Emma King was dead.

Almost immediately a great surge of anger made him raise both hands high over his head as though preparing to deliver a powerful blow to Emma's corpse and smash it. He checked himself just in time, but he was still beside himself. What right had this girl to come and die in his house and plunge him into trouble and possible disaster? His whole life had been a struggle to succeed: a struggle against desperate odds. Where was she when he was struggling with his studies? Where was she when he was burning the midnight oil and depriving himself of all those pleasures that his contemporaries were enjoying? Where was she? Where was she when he was working overtime, staying in his office after hours to master all those files so that the wheels of administration moved smoothly? Where was this useless little girl? And what right had she to make eyes at him at that so-called 'Sunday School'. If only he had not responded to those eyes. He should have known; he should have known what she was up to: seeking to entrap and bring down a man of substance who had spent decades struggling, planning, starving, studying hard, working himself to the bone to put his life together and make some kind of mark on the world. To think that all his labor should come to this!

Thus the panic-stricken Jedi reasoned in his anguish. But why did she die? What made her die? He had heard of people dying during sex, but they were usually males, and the cause of death was almost always a heart attack. He had never heard of a woman, much less a girl, dying during sex. The thing was unthinkable. And then he remembered the powerful orgasm that had made him grab her with all his might as he roared his fulfilment. Could it be that he had grabbed her by the throat? Could he have strangled her? A new flush of cold sweat swept over his still naked body as he considered the very real possibility that he might have killed her himself. If indeed he had held her by the throat with both hands and with all that strength in his powerful body, it was quite possible that he had strangled her. He now remembered the seemingly endless spasms that convulsed Emma's body as he went through his climax. At the time, he thought they constituted her own climax. Could they have been the convulsions of a girl being strangled? And that long gasping sigh, could that have been her last breath?

"Oh my God, I must have killed her!" he wailed, and beat his head against the bedpost. "I must have killed her!"

In a daze, he sat back on the bed, his eyes trained on the corpse. For a moment it seemed as if the whole room was swirling round. Then his head suddenly felt weightless; in fact, his whole body felt weightless, as though he were not really there. Perhaps the whole thing was a nightmare from which he would soon wake up. To steady himself, he grabbed his head with both hands, shut his eyes hard, then gradually reopened them. His head now felt quite steady and he was wide awake. But the corpse was still there. It was all too real!

What to do? In this kind of situation the normal thing would be to pick up the telephone and report the death to the police. After that, it would be left to the police. "The police!" Jedi almost screamed out, "Dear God! Not the police". Like all men of his status, Jedi considered members of the Sierra Leone police force to be dishonest and mercenary. This was just the kind of case that they prayed for: one involving a killing. Since he was a senior government official, they would not beat him up or torture him as they often did to suspects lower down the social ladder; but they would continually keep the prospect of the gallows hanging before his eyes and use it to milk him dry. He would become their milk cow, their source of sustenance for the next several months. Some of them would even pretend to be on his side, to be sorry for him and prepared to help him escape the clutches of the law and the gallows. But they would be the very ones who would milk him most mercilessly. And then, of course, they would laugh at him behind his back and tell all sorts of anecdotes and jokes against him. No! Definitely not the police!

The gallows! Had the idea of the gallows actually crossed his mind? Yes, it had. For the first time Jedi realized that he might be in actual danger of the gallows. God Almighty! How did he get himself into this mess? He who had always been such an upright, prim, proper, abstemious, law-abiding member of society! How did he contrive to bring himself into a situation in which he was in danger of the gallows? But it was an accident. He had certainly not intended to kill the girl. How could he kill a girl he liked so much, who had given him so much pleasure, and would no doubt have continued to give him indescribable pleasure had she lived? The thing looked very bad, he had to admit. A dead girl naked in his bed. It would lead to a tremendous scandal, tremendous disgrace. But her death was no gallows matter. The dumbest person should be able to see that. Any fair-minded society would realize that. But his next thought made him almost jump out of his skin.

How would society really see the situation? He forced himself to think about it calmly and objectively. Here was a naked girl, dead in his bed. She could have died after the sexual act; but she could also have died during the act. If that was the case, did he kill her? Once more those orgasmic convulsions came into Jedi's mind. Did he strangle her? If he strangled her, then he must have killed her. But even so, it was an accident.... Jedi could not bear the thought of having to explain to a policeman that he had strangled his lover at the height of passion. Imagine the guffaws of laughter! And even if he could bring himself to give this kind of explanation, would they believe him? Definitely not! He could imagine the headlines: "Middle-aged bachelor rapes and strangles teenaged girl!" Yes! That was how it would appear to everyone. Or that was the kind of sensational veneer the press would lay over the matter. They would never believe that Emma had slept with him voluntarily. They would decide that he tried to seduce her, and when she seemed unwilling, raped and then strangled her to prevent her telling. That would put his head in the noose as surely as night follows day. He would be seen as a monster, a great, big, black, gorilla of a monster who had dragged a defenseless seventeen-year-old girl to his bed, ravished her innocence, and then mercilessly snuffed the life out of her, with those powerful paws. God in heaven! Could a gentle, law-abiding, highly-principled citizen like him be presented in those monstrous colors? Yes! It was perfectly possible! The press could do it; the police could do it. No! He couldn't go to the police!

And yet something had to be done, and done quickly. The undeniable fact was that he had a dead girl in his bed. He had to think, to do something fast. Perhaps he should call up a close friend and ask for his advice and help. It was only then that Jedi realized with something of a shock that he did not have any really close friends apart from his mother. In his determination to succeed he had had little time to go partying with friends and besides, most of his contemporaries had married and developed other interests. He had no close relatives either: no brothers and sisters, and he had never cultivated the friendship of his first cousins. Perhaps he should contact Roger Neal, a brilliant lawyer who had been his classmate at university. He had been highly impressed with the efficient way in which Neal had dealt with a villainous youngster who had blackmailed one of Jedi's office mates. Yes! He would contact Neal. He would certainly be able to help with the legal aspects of the problem.

But there was still the problem of the body. It would have to be taken to the mortuary and handed over to her relations for burial and the whole thing would come out and become public property. He was absolutely certain that whomever he told of his predicament would advise him to go to the police or to inform Emma's relatives. And he would not be able to pull back. Once he told anyone, the thing would become public knowledge even if the person refused to help him. He could not afford to let the public know anything. Imagine what would happen when members of his church found out that he had not only had sex with a teenager, but that the girl had died in his bed! Imagine what his fellow sidesmen and committee members would say! Imagine what the members of the Mothers' Union would say! Some of them might even wonder if he had been secretly having affairs with their own adolescent daughters. Imagine what the vicar would say! He would never be able to show his face in the church again. How could he bear to forgo the church fellowship; the pleasantries exchanged every Sunday after the morning service; the glorious church celebrations and festivals in which he, as People's Warden, played such an important part; and the respect and adulation that were always accorded to him! How could he forgo strutting up the aisle every Sunday as the file of wardens and sidesmen made their distinguished way to the altar to present the people's offerings to the Lord, his head held high; his crisply pressed morning dress exuding dignity, good breeding and prosperity. How could he be expected to forgo all that?

And if the thing became public knowledge he might even have to give up his job and all the perks and privileges that went with it. He would have to say goodbye to further promotion and to further preferment. He would almost certainly have to give up all thoughts of the Mastership of his Masonic Lodge, that he and everyone else thought should be his by right and due process of succession. He had even begun to entertain thoughts of the University conferring an honorary doctorate on him in the not too distant future. After all, they had conferred honorary degrees on less deserving people. So why not on him? If the thing became known he would have to forget about that. He would have to forgo membership of the Board of Governors of his Alma Mater. He would have to forgo membership of the executive of the Young Men's Christian Association. He would be reduced to an absolute nonentity, unemployed and possibly poor, that is if he did not go to jail into the bargain. Jail! The thought of going to jail made his flesh creep. This would be the height of disgrace and degradation. It would be a stigma that he would never be able to get rid of even if his imprisonment was short. And to think that he would have to mingle with all those murderers and thieves and rapists, that he would have to sleep in bug and roach-infested quarters and put up with the stench and filth of the common toilet! To think he would have to eat the disgusting mess that no doubt passed for prison food! Oh God! Not jail! He could not afford to go to jail. He would not be able to stand it. He would rather die.

And then yet another thought struck him. Here he was thinking about jail when, in all probability, he might end up being sentenced to death if the thing became known. Yes! He was in danger of the gallows, not just of jail. Once again Jedi broke into a cold sweat and his heart started pounding wildly. *God! I am innocent! I haven't done anything* he thought, pounding the bed with his fists. *God, you know I am innocent!*

But he also knew that to be innocent in the sight of God was one thing; to be innocent in the eyes of the police and a human court was quite another.

The thought of all that could happen made him get to his feet. As he continued to consider his predicament, he went downstairs to his drinks cabinet, got out a bottle of whisky and poured himself a stiff drink. Normally, Jedi seldom drank strong liquor and only kept whisky and brandy in the house because a man in his position was expected to have spirits in the house. However, on such a night, he felt he needed the whisky to steady his nerves. Indeed, he felt bolder, stronger, ready to face and plan anything as soon as the potent liquid had coursed through his veins. This was good. He poured himself another and downed it in one go. Now to think and plan, he said to himself, deciding to remain downstairs while he did so. The thought of facing Emma's corpse was simply unbearable.

First of all, he pursued what he called the logic of the situation. If no one must know, then the body could not be returned to the relatives. No one must know that the girl had died, let alone that she had died in his place. Fortunately, no one knew that she had come to visit him. Even if she had told her friends that she was coming to visit him, which was unlikely, there would be nothing to suggest that something had happened to her at his place. She could have gone somewhere else and been killed, or she could have been kidnapped or something. Even if his old busybody of a neighbor had seen Emma coming into his compound, which he also thought highly unlikely, she did not know her identity and would not necessarily link any missing girl with a girl she saw entering the compound of Mr. Jedi Thomas. No, he was covered from that angle too. So all he now needed to do was to dispose of the body himself. Certainly, the girl's relatives would miss her, the police might even be persuaded to emerge from their lethargy and mount a search, but it would not be possible to link Emma's disappearance with him. He would have to steel himself to deny all knowledge of her if the need arose. Yes that was it. He would have to dispose of the body somehow, without any assistance.

But how was he to dispose of the body? This was a difficult problem and in order to think it out clearly, Jedi poured himself another stiff drink. Couldn't he just dump it into some kind of open lavatory? He had heard of young girls dumping their new-born babies into open latrines. A latrine seemed to him the natural place for dumping a corpse. Since everyone expected that kind of latrine to give off a horrible smell, nobody would bother about the stench. Perhaps that was what he ought to do. But then it occurred to him that there was a world of difference between a six-pound baby and a seventeen year-old girl, five feet two inches tall. How on earth would he get her into the latrine by himself? And, in any case, where would he find such a latrine? There would be open latrines in the nearby villages, but he couldn't just drag a body into someone's compound, enter the latrine, prime the wooden top off with a crowbar, topple the body in and replace the top. It would be too risky.

Couldn't he burn the body? He had a big compound behind his house where the cremation could be done. He could drag the body down into a corner of his compound in the dead of night, douse it with petrol, and set it alight. He had read somewhere of a sixty-two year old mother-in-law in England, sometime in the fifties or sixties, who burnt her daughter-in-law's body after she had murdered her. The woman had been caught and hanged. But that was probably because, being a woman, and an elderly one at that, she had probably been incapable of thinking as logically as he was doing now. He would have to ensure that he did not leave tell-tale evidence. But how could he avoid that? Someone was bound to see the fire, especially if he used petrol. Then there might be some tell-tale evidence left, like bones. There was also the real possibility that if he used petrol he might set his own and other people's property on fire. What about wood? He would need a lot of wood, and he would have to buy it from someone, which could be used as evidence against him later. The body might start to decompose while he collected the wood and the game would be up. Moreover, a cremation using wood would take far too long. No! Cremation was out. It was just as well that the whisky was making him think so clearly that he was able to rule out these risky alternatives to dumping the body.

In the end, he decided to load Emma's body into the trunk of his car in the dead of night, take it to some remote place, and throw it either into the sea or into the bush. He settled on the bush when he remembered that bodies thrown into the sea sometimes got washed ashore. He would drive along the Peninsula road, park his car in some remote spot, take the body into the bush and leave it there. No one would be any the wiser. He felt he could now face the corpse again, so having replenished his glass of whisky, he made his way back upstairs, congratulating himself for the cool and methodical way he had thought out a solution to his problem. He would soon dispose of the body, and be able to continue with his life as if nothing had happened. No chit of a girl, who wasn't even born when he started his struggles, would be allowed to mar his life or divert it from its chosen course. From now on Emma King would merely be a footnote in his history, a brief though exciting and enjoyable interlude.

Jedi looked at the clock on his bedside table. It was now nine thirty-five: two and a half hours since Emma died in his arms. How quickly time had flown! He supposed this was because his brain had been so busy working out the solution to his problem. But timing was now critically important. He would have to take the body out when there were very few people about; one could not be too cautious. If something should go wrong down the line he wanted to be able to deny that he was out with his car at any time during this night. Therefore, the fewer people who saw him, the better. So he would have to set out well after midnight, probably about two in the morning. But that meant that he would have to find some means of passing the next four and a half hours. Four and a half hours! Would he have to be looking at that corpse for four and a half hours, watching it get progressively stiffer and colder? At this thought, he glanced at Emma's face. Her eyes were half open, but her mouth, which had remained agape since he gave her those powerful shakes, seemed to be accusing him. A fly was already hovering around those lips that had been such a source of pleasure! Now, with the fly hovering around, he imagined that a stench was already emanating from them and he closed them quickly. Thus, he performed with disgust an act normally performed with love by bereaved relatives.

As he continued to look down at Emma's body, Jedi began to wonder how on earth he could have been infatuated with this girl. Her body now looked so grotesque that it even seemed to mock the sexual act. Even her face had begun to lose its lustre and attractiveness. He rushed to a closet adjacent to his wardrobe and got out a white bed-sheet with which he hastily covered the body from head to toe, not because it was the decent thing to do, but because it revolted him. He couldn't help thinking that this was Emma's shroud, and this was her laying-out, a grotesque laying-out, before her burial.

The idea of the shroud brought a related question into his mind. Should he dress the body up again or should he bury it naked? He certainly was not going to bury it in the sheet. If anything went wrong, it might be traced to him. Jedi looked at the uniform, at the pink knickers and white slip that Emma had carelessly thrown over a chair before she climbed into his bed, and at the shoes at the foot of the chair. He could not bring himself to put all those items back on the body. He would dress it only in the uniform, for decency's sake. He could not just throw her away naked into the bush, like a dog! Resolving not to look at the face, he uncovered the corpse, raised the body by the shoulders and tried to slip the uniform over its head. The process was much more difficult than he had supposed. Not realizing that the gradually stiffening arms would offer tremendous resistance, he had imagined that dressing the corpse would be like dressing a little child. Making matters worse, the face seemed determined to stare at him. After several attempts, Jedi gave up, laid the body down and covered it up again with the sheet. He would have to bury it naked. That was the logical conclusion.

Once again, he complimented himself on how clearly his mind was working in the midst of a crisis. He knew what he would do: bury the body in one of the empty rice bags he had in the kitchen cupboard. In fact, he thought, it was a good idea not to dress it in the uniform after all. That way it would not be easy to identify if it were ever found.

He rushed downstairs again and got out one of the rice bags and a coil of thick white rope about two feet long. Once more in his bedroom, he removed the sheet, raised the body from the bed and thrust it naked into the bag, head first. Then he quickly tied up the bag. It occurred to him that he might as well take it downstairs at once and put it into the trunk of his car. He could then come back upstairs and rest for a while, perhaps even sleep, until it was time for him to set about the task of disposing of the body. That way, he would not have to sit and stare at all that remained of his one-time lover.

To get into the garage, Jedi did not need to go outside as there was a door leading to it directly from his kitchen. And since the outside door was always locked, no one would see him taking the body downstairs and putting it into the trunk of the car. He mentally congratulated himself on the excellence of his house's design which he attributed to his own intelligence. It amazed him that most people never thought of all the ways in which particular aspects of the building could be useful when designing a house. As he hoisted the bag onto his shoulders, his knees almost gave way beneath its weight, but he steadied himself and proceeded to struggle down the stairs. How could such a tiny girl weigh so much, he wondered.

However, once in the garage, everything was easy. Emma's body fitted easily into the commodious trunk of his car that had become a makeshift hearse.

Jedi decided not to switch the garage light on, just in case someone watching from outside or from a neighbor's window, might remember that there was light in his garage on this particular night. In any case, he knew his way around his garage and around his car. He momentarily remembered with an involuntary shudder, the Biblical saying his mother had often quoted to him when he was young: "Men love darkness rather than light because their deeds are evil." But he reasoned that he was not doing anything wrong because he had not really murdered the girl. He had not intended to kill her, and in getting rid of the body like this, he was merely protecting himself and his reputation.

As he positioned the body in the trunk, a dazzling flash of lightning rent the night sky. It lit up the garage and shone on the rice bag, highlighting its whiteness. Tremendous fear gripped Jedi and he shuddered again. Immediately after the lightning, came a sharp, splitting sound and all the lights went out. Jedi was thrown into a panic although he did not quite know why. He would not have called himself superstitious, but he did believe in the power of the supernatural and even in black magic and African science. Could it be that some malignant force disapproved of his actions and was trying to expose the deed in spite of his caution and secrecy? He bounded up the stairs and by the time he reached his bedroom, he was once again bathed in sweat. And then came the inevitable peal of thunder like the sound of heavy artillery pounding some neighborhood into submission. Jedi could hear several of his neighbors screaming as the force of the thunder rattled their glassware, crockery, furniture, and other possessions. It was almost as though the malignant force Jedi had thought of had taken hold of the whole neighborhood and was shaking it out of its senses. Jedi jumped on to his bed as if it would offer him protection against the malignant power. However, he had not been lying there for more than a few seconds when he heard something sharp knocking against the windowpanes. His first thought was that someone had seen him in spite of all his precautions. But then it occurred to him that no one could be knocking against his bedroom window, because the window was quite a long way from the ground. Could it be Emma's ghost then, trying to get at him? Although he was normally a brave man, Jedi shivered in fright. It was only after a while that he realized that what he had heard were heavy raindrops beating against the windowpane.

And then the rain came down in torrents. It was the heaviest downpour that Jedi could remember. It was easy to believe that whatever gods or demons were responsible for guarding the rain barrels up in the sky had decided to break all of them open and dash the contents on to the unsuspecting earth. It was worse than a downpour; it was becoming a terrific storm. He could hear the wind howling like so many demented ghosts as it made its way from the Atlantic on to Juba Hill. Once it reached his house it swirled around it, roaring and snarling, demanding to be let in, threatening to rip the roof off and thrust itself in by force. The wind's behavior put Jedi in mind of dogs which had followed a strong scent and were absolutely sure that their prey was lodged within. They wouldn't budge or cease their howling until the unfortunate victim was either apprehended or torn to pieces. Yes, this storm was like a bloody policeman who had come for him with vicious German shepherd dogs. As it continued to rage, Jedi huddled towards the foot of the bed as though to avoid being seen or being hit by powerful blows. But the brilliant flashes of lightning continued relentlessly, and each flash exposed him, lying huddled on the bed, shivering like a cornered culprit. To make matters worse, the flashes of lightning also lit up Emma's clothes, still resting on the chair, and her shoes at the foot of the chair. Whenever Jedi saw them, he shivered even more. The storm had almost completely eroded the confidence he had felt up to half an hour ago. Once again, he began to see himself as a guilty person who might soon have to face judgment. Perhaps the storm itself was God's expression of anger for the vile act he had committed; perhaps it was God's instrument for uncovering the monstrous deed and the identity of the perpetrator, in which case, he was done for.

"Mercy! Dear God, mercy!" he whimpered, still huddled at the foot of the bed. "Let not this sin weigh heavily against me today, oh Lord, not today. Have mercy, and forgive, Lord!"

But the storm continued unabated, and in its accents Jedi could hear a thousand devils clamoring for his soul and a thousand ghost-hounds howling for his blood. Once more he asked himself, *How did I ever get myself into this mess?* He had not intended to harm anybody. Why should this be happening to him? Why should he be in such a situation? These self-pitying thoughts reminded him that there was a body in the trunk of his car and he had to get rid of it. God in heaven! It was already two in the morning! He would have to make a move, but the storm showed no sign of abating. Could he go out in such weather? What if the storm continued until the morning and he had not been able to get rid of the body by then? His houseboy arrived for work at seven in the morning. He himself would have to leave for work by eight. Could he take the risk of leaving his houseboy alone in the house with a body in it? But the body was already in the trunk of his car. Could he travel in the car with a body in the trunk? What if some thief primed his trunk open and found a body there? What if the body started to decompose and give off a stench? No! He would have to get rid of the body before morning, even if that meant venturing out into the storm. On further reflection he realized that the weather would serve his purpose well, for it would ensure that there would be no one else on the road. Even the watchmen working for the nearby households would be taking cover on such a night. Only people with the worst kinds of purposes would be abroad on a night that would scare even devils into hiding.

With this new line of reasoning, his confidence started to return, and he decided to leave right away. He threw on some clothes and a pair of sneakers, grabbed his bunch of keys and some money. One never knew! The money would come in handy in the unlikely event of his meeting someone who might need to be bribed into silence. In any case, a 'big' man ought always to go out with money in his pocket. He had almost left his bedroom when it occurred to him that he would need some protection against the fury of the elements, since he would have to get out of the car at some point. So he found his gray plastic raincoat, then made his way carefully downstairs in the dark. Once in his garage he was tempted to check and see whether the body was still in the trunk, but resisted the urge. He would not look at that body again unless he needed to. Having opened the garage door and his main gate as quietly as he could, he started the engine and emerged from his compound with as little noise as possible. Thinking that on a night like this, not even thieves would be out, he didn't bother to get out of the car again and close the main gate,

His car, a black Mercedes, made its slow way down Juba Hill. Jedi felt as if he were driving a hearse in which a corpse was commencing its journey to its final resting place. The car's progress was necessarily slow not only because Jedi wanted to make as little noise as possible, but also because of the violence of the storm. Although he had not wound down the windows, Jedi could hear the storm howling around it. His windscreen wipers were going at full speed, but there was little they could do to keep off the sheets of water that lashed against the glass, blinding him. Once he reached the main road and turned left towards Goderich village, he discovered that the road was rapidly becoming a river, and there was a distinct possibility that his car would be swept away. Visibility was reduced to about twenty feet, but, he had to plod on regardless.

Jedi drove on at about fifteen miles an hour, and he did not see or encounter a single creature or sign of life along the way. However, his normal confidence and courage had reasserted themselves and he drove on without fear. His mind registered the devastation that the storm had already caused. Several enormous trees had been uprooted, their huge multifarious roots exposed. Several telephone, electric and telegraph poles were down or were slanted at angles varying from sixty to twenty degrees from the base. And the river of water that used to be the road now carried all kinds of debris.

Jedi drove for more than an hour, looking for a suitable spot. He had originally intended to drive beyond York before attempting to get rid of the body, his argument being that the further away from Freetown he deposited the body, the less likely it was to be found, and in the unlikely event of its being found, the less likely it was for it to be linked with him. But going beyond York in this kind of weather would be suicidal. He had already negotiated some death-threatening bridges and knew that the dreaded Comfort Bridge was only a few miles from York. Traversing it in the best of weathers and in broad daylight was dangerous enough; he would be taking his life in his hands if he attempted to do so in such a storm and in pitch darkness. He would have to choose a spot just before he reached Comfort Bridge. As it happened, the decision was taken out of Jedi's hands, for about a mile from the bridge, he noticed that the Mercedes was swerving slightly although he was going so slowly. Then he observed the car making a kind of lopsided motion.

Jedi was sufficiently experienced to know exactly what was happening and his heart thumped wildly. Of all days and nights in the year, what a time to have a puncture! What on earth was he to do now? Should he get out and try to change the tire? Would he be able to in this kind of storm and in pitch darkness? He remembered that he always had a torch in his glove compartment. But a torch was useless unless there was someone to hold it for him while he worked.

The solution dawned on him as clearly as the lightning that had so brightly illuminated the rice bag in the trunk of his car. This was the very spot that he needed. It was remote, with jungle on both sides of the road. He reckoned it was about eighteen miles or so from Freetown. Yes! He would find somewhere deep in the bush to bury the body, then return to change the tire at his leisure and return home. The storm might even have abated by then. Everything seemed to be working together for good, he thought gladly. Maybe the flat tire was the work of Providence; maybe it was intended to reveal to him exactly where he was to dispose of the body. Maybe it was a kind of safeguard to ensure that the car was not stolen while he was away burying the body in the bush. Yes! Providence itself was directing him. He took the torch from the glove compartment, got out of the car, locked it, then went to the trunk. As he opened it, another flash of lightning lit up the bag in the trunk, showing the outlines of the body within it. Jedi shuddered again and in his panic almost let the trunk slam shut. But he revved up his courage, and slowly withdrew both the body and a spade he had brought with him. Hoisting both on to his shoulders, he closed the trunk and started his laborious journey into the bush. As he took the first step, a peal of thunder boomed out, sounding as if a gigantic bell were tolling for Emma as her corpse entered the graveyard.

The downpour had seemed to abate a little when Jedi got out of the car, but after the thunder, it lashed down again with renewed vigor. The wind continued to howl and moan. To Jedi's ears, it now sounded ghostly and lugubrious. The burden on his shoulders seemed to grow heavier and heavier as he slowly made his way into the dark and menacing jungle. His plastic raincoat was proving quite incapable of keeping the water from his clothes and his person, and he had no covering for his head. The soggy ground under his feet further slowed down his progress, but he plodded on, wanting to go as far from the road as possible before digging a grave. It would have to be a shallow one, because he had neither the energy nor the time to dig a proper grave in the sodden earth. His progress was further impeded by the thickness of the undergrowth and the many creepers and tendrils which wrapped themselves around his feet as if determined to hold him fast until daylight appeared and humans came to arrest him. He had to kick against them with all his might. However, he found himself being somewhat grateful to the storm because it had ensured that most of the wild animals and annoying insects had taken cover. He was also glad that the near total darkness made it hard to discern the more awesome trees. Another brilliant flash of lightning revealed the brown outline of something long and slender in the undergrowth, inches from his right foot. Jedi jumped, giving a tremendous shout. He landed on his left foot, slipped in the mud and went crashing to the ground with his burden. His torch slipped out of his hand and went out, rendering the darkness total. Panting with exhaustion and fear, and maddened with renewed rage, he groped around in the dark for the torch. It was a good ten minutes before he found it. Thank goodness it still worked. He now realized that in falling he had wounded his left arm on the edge of the spade. He managed to replace his burden on his shoulders through the gnawing pain, and continued his funereal march, struggling against the undergrowth, the wind and the rain.

It took another fifteen minutes before another sudden flash of lightning showed him that he had arrived just at the edge of a rather deep gully. Yes! This weather had, in a sense, been a godsend. Without the lightning he would probably have fallen into the gully, and who could tell whether he would have been able to get out of it or whether he would not have been so disabled by the fall that he would have had to stay there until wild animals or birds of prey came and devoured him?

With the aid of his torch, Jedi saw that the sides of the gully were steep. In this weather, he thought, there was probably a small stream at the bottom of it. Tree branches reached across it on either side, meeting in the middle to form flimsy bridges which reminded Jedi of the grave he had seen at a Muslim funeral. After the body had been taken out of the bier and laid at the bottom of the grave, it was covered over with wooden planks; then slim tree branches were piled on, before earth was heaped on the body. The recollection gave him an idea. Why bother to dig a grave in this most inclement of weathers when there was one ready to hand? If he could somehow get Emma's body to the bottom of this gully, the overhanging trees and branches would ensure that no one ever found it. Of course, there was the drawback that it might be discovered by wild animals and devoured, but...

Another dazzling flash of lightning lit up the whole of the sky, the whole of the forest, and was so terrifying that Jedi's courage finally deserted him. He cried out as though he were being stabbed to his very heart. It was a shout of despair and of defiance, announcing that he had had enough. With a fierce movement, he raised his burden high above his head and sent it hurtling towards the depths of the gully. Some of the intertwined branches over the gully broke the bundle's fall as it hit them, but came together once more, hiding the evidence. And then the thunder boomed its final requiem: a heavy, long-drawn-out drum-roll. With a huge sigh of relief, the only human witness of poor Emma's obsequies turned away from her grave.

CHAPTER 3

Whenever he thought about it later, Jedi could not explain how he managed to find his way out of the forest and back to the road in that storm. He must have struggled with the undergrowth, with the sodden earth, and with creepers and treacherous pools, while the wind howled mournfully around him and the thunder growled overhead, yet he could not remember any details of the experience. He later attributed his successful exit to his will to live, and to his desire to put as great a distance as possible, and as fast as possible, between himself and the corpse he had just 'buried': between himself and his crime.

When he reached the road once more, he felt as if he had just woken up from a deep sleep or had been roused from a trance, or as if he had just been restored to sobriety after a drunken stupor. His head, hands and feet felt as though they did not really belong to his body, as though his own had been taken from him and he had borrowed others belonging to someone much bigger and heavier. Once more, the desperate wish returned that the whole thing had been a nightmare. But he looked at the road and saw his car there, as solid a sign as any that the experience he had just gone through was not a nightmare, but was all too real. It was only then that he remembered that one of his tires had suffered a puncture just before he went into the bush. At first, he thought of sleeping out the rest of the storm and the night in the car; help was sure to come in the morning. That way he would be able to get much needed rest. On second thoughts, however, he decided it was a bad idea. Whatever happened, he must be nowhere near this place when morning came. That would surely tie him to the murder if the body were found. At the very least, he would have to account for his being so far from his home in such a desolate and remote area, and in such dreadful weather. No! He would have to press on and change the tire himself.

Unlike many other senior civil servants, Jedi did not always depend on messengers or houseboys to change tires for him. He did not mind soiling his hands and had often done the job himself. However, changing a car tire in such devilish weather was another matter. He was already soaked to the skin, so he had nothing to lose by exposing himself to another few inches of rain; but the night was as black as pitch and he needed to be able to see in order to do the job properly; he could hardly hold the torch in one hand and work with the other. Damn that blasted girl! He was paying much too high a price for the fleeting moments of pleasure he had had with her. However, Jedi soon found that he could solve his immediate problem by supporting the lighted torch in the cleft of a small tree by the roadside and angling it in such a way that the light focused on the tire in question, the one on the right and at the back.

Once he started the mechanical process of changing the tire, he found it was really quite easy after all. That was the beauty of having a Mercedes, he thought smugly. Everything in it had been designed to make things easy for its owner. The wheel nuts came off easily and the hydraulic jack soon raised the right side of the car to the required height. The flat tire also came off and was replaced with the spare without any difficulty. He was then able to lower the car, remove the jack and tighten the nuts with little more than a flick of his finger. How easy it had been! Perhaps that was a good omen.

It was only after Jedi entered the car to commence what he imagined would be the grueling journey home that he realized that the storm had abated as suddenly as it had started. The rain had almost ceased, so the windscreen wipers had much less water to wipe than previously. The fog had also lifted and visibility was now almost one hundred per cent. This was another good omen. In any case, it meant that he would be able to drive home much faster. What else could this mean other than that Emma's death and burial were firmly behind him and everything would be all right? He had frustrated and defeated the forces of nature by sheer determination and strength of will. That was how a man should behave. That was how he had always behaved. *Set a goal and reach for it and don't allow yourself to be deterred even by the devil himself.* This had always been the secret of his success. And now he had triumphed once more. As he started his homeward journey, he could see faint signs of dawn already appearing in the distance. That was also a good omen. Yes! He had really put the darkness behind him. Emma had been a distraction, a diversion from the normal pattern of his life. He would forget her completely, and return to the even tenor of his life.

Once he got home, Jedi raced upstairs to his bedroom, grateful that electric power had been restored. His bedside clock told him the time was a quarter to six. Having changed his clothes and dried himself quickly, he was about to flop on to his bed when he noticed Emma's clothes and beret on the chair and her shoes on the floor. Damn that girl! How dare she intrude herself on his attention again when he thought he was finally rid of her? He would have to dispose of her clothes and shoes immediately. Collecting them, he went down to his car, siphoned petrol from the tank, dug a hole in a sheltered and unpaved area to the back of the house, put Emma's belongings into it, and set them alight. A tremendous blaze flared immediately, but since it was so early in the morning, Jedi was fairly certain that none of his neighbors would observe it from their windows. Even if they did, they were probably superstitious enough to conclude that he was carrying out some ceremony prescribed by a medicine man. Let them think what they liked. In a few minutes, the clothes and the beret were nothing but a pile of ash. The shoes were more stubborn, but that didn't worry him; everything would soon be buried. He filled up the hole with earth, smoothed it over, stamped it down and breathed a sigh of relief. The last of Emma King had finally been obliterated from the earth and he could now sleep peacefully. He went back upstairs, covered himself securely with his blanket, and fell into a deep sleep.

He was jolted out of his slumber at about seven in the morning by the ringing of the bell at his front gate. At first, he heard it as though from a long distance away, a tinkling sound that merely troubled his semi-consciousness. But its persistence roused him into full consciousness, and he realized that it must be his steward, Juldeh, arriving at his usual time. Jedi's eyelids felt heavy and his whole body ached as if several witches had beaten him all night with broomsticks. However, he rubbed his eyes, stretched and yawned, sat up in bed, checked the time, then dragged himself out of bed to let Juldeh in.

****

Juldeh was a handsome, lively, twenty-one-year-old Foulah who had made his way to Freetown from neighboring Guinea three years before in search of a better life. According to him, life in Guinea was extremely tough, especially for uneducated people like himself. So like droves of other young male Guineans, he had made his way south of the border. He knew that, given his illiteracy and lack of any kind of skill, the best he could hope for was work as a houseboy, but he did not mind doing this until he had saved enough money to buy some goods and convert himself into a street trader. From that small beginning, he saw himself moving on to owning his own shop, and then the sky would be the limit. Or he could buy himself an apprenticeship with one of the leading Guinean tailors. He knew that once he learned to sew, his fortune would be made.

Juldeh had not found it so easy to gain employment as a houseboy. The economic situation in his new country meant that fewer people were employing stewards, and those who were did not seem to wish to employ him because of a mistaken impression that Foulahs could not be trusted. Eventually, Juldeh had the good fortune to be introduced to Jedi. From his own experience, Jedi had found that, contrary to popular prejudice, Foulahs were not only neat and hardworking, but also quite honest. He had been sorry when his previous steward left him to become a street trader, so Juldeh was exactly the replacement he had been looking for. As he expected, Juldeh was efficient and quick to learn. He became invaluable, not only as gardener and general cleaner, but also as cook. Besides, Juldeh was always optimistic, always in high spirits, and always ready to regale Jedi with the latest news, which Jedi usually thoroughly enjoyed listening to.

On this particular morning Juldeh was absolutely bubbling over with excitement, and he had hardly stepped into the compound and greeted his master when he blurted out:

"Boss, that was a wonderful breeze, last night! I can't find the mouth to describe it."

Quite oblivious of the look of alarm that came over his employer's face the moment he introduced the subject, he nonetheless went on to describe the storm in graphic terms.

"That tornado was frightening, boss! People are saying they have not seen anything like it for the last twenty years. Boss, you should see the town! There are trees all over the place. I tried to count the ones that had been blown down and that I saw with my own two eyeballs. After a while I gave up; they were too many. And the roofs of so many houses have been blown away! You know old Pa Thompson at Smart Farm? The breeze blew his roof far, far away. They did not find even one sheet of corrugated iron, or one piece of board. The rain beat down on Pa Thompson as he was sleeping in his bed. And you know the big compound lower down the hill with the big mango trees? Pa Temple's place. One of the trees fell down on the house and smashed it to pieces. I'll be surprised if someone did not die..."

Still unaware of Jedi's expression, Juldeh babbled on.

"Boss, this night was God's wonder! Some people are saying that it was not an ordinary breeze. They say this kind of breeze does not happen for nothing and we will soon hear an announcement that some big man has died or has got into serious trouble. With the election coming, all sorts of strange things are happening these days. I even hear that some people have disappeared without..."

After recent events, it was too much for Jedi. Without realizing it, or even intending it, Juldeh had touched a nerve with all that talk about a big man dying or getting into some kind of trouble, and about people disappearing.

"Just shut your big mouth and go about your work!" he ordered.

The unusual harshness of that response surprised Jedi himself, and as for Juldeh, his employer's unusual hostility came as a bombshell almost as devastating as the storm. Relations between master and servant had been most cordial, even familiar up till then. Jedi had always allowed him to rattle on and on and on every morning to his heart's content. Juldeh simply could not understand what had got into his master that morning. Maybe the storm had affected him in some way. Maybe it had prevented him from sleeping soundly. Yes! That must be it! His eyes looked heavy and he seemed tired, like someone who had just returned from a long and exhausting journey. Juldeh thought it prudent to go into the kitchen and begin his daily chores.

Through his open front door, Jedi now took in the devastation the storm had caused. It was almost as though a bomb had been dropped on his part of town. As Juldeh had told him, several houses were without roofs and the roads were littered with debris: tree leaves and branches, pieces of board that had helped to hold roofs in place, twisted sheets of corrugated iron, and poles that once held up electric wires or parts of buildings. It was one enormous mess. Jedi looked with pity at several people who must have been made practically homeless and who were trying to salvage whatever they could out of the wreckage. Yes! It had been a terrible night. Could it possibly have been connected to the crime he had committed? Was it the protest of the elements against what he had done? Had the elements been trying to get at him? If so, he had escaped. And, he noted with satisfaction, his house had hardly been touched; but it was just as well he had decided to move that girl's body when he did. It would have been disastrous if his roof had been blown off to reveal her corpse on his bed. Yes, he had been very lucky. He would deposit a special thank-offering envelope in the collection plate when he went to church next Sunday, in gratitude for his deliverance. He would also send up his name for a special prayer of thanksgiving.

These thoughts greatly comforted Jedi, and he was in relatively high spirits as he made his way back to his bedroom. He decided that he was too tired to go to work that morning, so he told Juldeh that he was feeling unwell and would be staying in bed for the rest of the day. *No wonder he shouted at me like that,* Juldeh said to himself, relieved that there was a reason for his employer's strange behavior. After eight o'clock, Jedi called his Secretary to say that owing to a sudden indisposition, he would not be coming to the office, then he went back to bed and straight to sleep.

By the following Sunday, three days later, Jedi had almost completely forgotten the incident. He had returned to work on Friday, greatly refreshed, and went about his duties as if nothing had happened. From his demeanor, none of his secretaries and typists would have guessed that he had recently gone through such a traumatic experience. Yes, he had resumed the even tenor of his life. It was only as he was about to leave for church early that Sunday morning that he was forcibly reminded of the incident. The sidesmen and sideswomen's annual thanksgiving service was taking place that day and special envelopes had, of course, been distributed. As People's Warden, he was one of the co-presidents of the organization and would naturally be expected to make a fat donation. It was while he was stuffing the money into the envelope that he remembered that he had resolved to make a special thank-offering that Sunday. He found a plain envelope, stuffed a substantial amount of money into it, and wrote on the front, "from J. Thomas, in gratitude." That done, he placed both envelopes into his inside pocket, relegated the incident once more to the back of his mind, and prepared to go and serve his maker.

On special Sundays, all the sidesmen were expected to turn out in European morning dress, complete with pinstriped trousers, locally known as trouselene, frock coats, matching waistcoats, matching ties, and winged collars. Jedi was particularly proud of his morning dress, which he had bought during one of his trips to London, from a store specializing in serving English barristers-at-law and other high-class people. His had been made to measure, so that it fitted him like a glove. With his imposing figure and handsome face, he knew he looked stunning in this garb. Indeed, when he arrived at the church and emerged from his Mercedes, he heard some youngsters letting out appreciative cries of "Wow!." That felt so good, confirming as it did, his position as a role model: someone whom the young people looked up to in that age of corruption and vice. Yes! It was good that in this age of depravity some youngsters still knew whom to look up to and admire. Jedi was completely in his element as he chatted with the sideswomen and other sidesmen, firmly giving instructions where necessary and putting the final touches to or reviewing the arrangements for the day with the Vicar, the Church Warden and Lay Readers. Nothing could have better confirmed his position and reputation. His opinion was consulted and he was listened to with deference and respect.

As People's Warden, it was Jedi's pleasant duty to escort Distinguished Grand Chief Patrons to their seats. That day, the distinguished personage was an honorable cabinet minister. In fact, he was the minister who had overall cabinet responsibility for Jedi's department, and so our hero was naturally anxious to make a good impression now that the Minister had an opportunity to see him in his religious setting. It was extremely important that the minister should feel that it was worth his while to be Distinguished Grand Chief Patron for such an occasion and that a tremendous boost had been given to his ego and reputation. Jedi was absolutely determined that this should be the case. His chances of enhancement might well depend on this. The government was always looking out for suitable people to send out as ambassadors or to appoint as chairmen or directors of corporations or as members of important boards. He fully intended that his name should keep coming up when such positions were being discussed. It was therefore important that he make the minister feel good. So when the Honorable Minister Distinguished Grand Chief Patron arrived, Jedi met him and his wife at the west door with the usual pleasantries, bowed obsequiously, shook hands most warmly and said,

"Can I have the extreme pleasure of escorting you and your lady wife to your seats, sir?"

"Of course! Of course! You lead, and we'll follow. Ha! Ha! Ha!"

Jedi could see some of the other sidesmen giving him envious looks. Well, that was the reward for his hard work and sacrifice. 'Seest thou a man diligent in his business, he shall stand before kings, and not before mean men,' or as the African proverb put it, 'If a child washes his hands properly, he can eat with elders.' He had washed his hands properly; that was why he was eating with elders. He had been diligent in his business; that was why he could hobnob with kings. The other sidesmen only had themselves to blame if they were not in his enviable position. So Jedi strutted ahead of the Honorable Minister and his lady wife, his face wreathed in self-satisfied smiles. The church was already quite full. There were other important people in the congregation who had been invited to be Patrons, Chief patrons and Grand Chief Patrons. All eyes were turned on Jedi and his minister. Jedi knew that the respect and admiration accorded the Honorable Minister rubbed on to him as well, so he strode slowly and with tremendous dignity right up to the end of the aisle, showed the Honorable Minister and his lady wife to the velvet padded front seats just left of the aisle, handed them their copies of the printed program, smiled graciously, bowed with due decorum, and cast his eyes all round the congregation before returning to the vestry.

The service itself turned out to be a huge success. Afterwards, several parishioners, guests, and church officers congratulated Jedi warmly. He was sure that this was because they all knew that the morning's success was almost entirely due to his brilliant organizational abilities. Yes, everything had gone very well indeed. The choir had sung a glorious anthem —'The Heavens are Telling the Glory of God,' no less: the kind of anthem that made one's hair stand on end. Almost every member of the congregation had gone up to the altar to deposit a thank-offering envelope, which meant that the morning's takings would be particularly substantial. Indeed, when Jedi and the Pastor's Warden later checked the offerings, they found that their honorable Distinguished Grand Chief Patron had donated one hundred thousand leones. *Yes!* Jedi thought, *that is how a big man should behave. Give a sum worthy of your exalted position, and make everyone respect and admire you more.* This generous donation also showed precisely in what high esteem the Minister held the person who had invited him to be the Distinguished Grand Chief Patron. Jedi was sure the point would not be lost on the Pastor's Warden and other sidesmen and sideswomen. The hymns had also been glorious and appropriate. He had relished 'Through all the changing scenes of life' particularly the verse that went, 'The hosts of God encamp around the dwellings of the just; deliverance He affords to all who on His succor trust.' So very appropriate. He felt as though the hymn was about his recent experiences. Had not God miraculously delivered him and saved him when all around him people were losing valuable belongings? Had not God delivered him when the forces of nature were doing their damnedest best to expose and frustrate him? And that verse was sung just as he was about to deposit his two envelopes into the collection plate. He had taken special care to ensure that those around him noticed that he was depositing two envelopes.

Yes, it had all gone rather well. The only slightly jarring note was caused by the excellent sermon on the text, 'Choose you this day whom you will serve, but as for me and my house, we will serve the Lord.' The Reverend Donald Peters had a great reputation as a sincere and inspirational preacher, and the congregation had responded to him with murmurs and nods of approbation. He expounded on the background to that biblical text and went on to relate it to the present occasion.

The church officers who were giving thanks to the Lord that day had chosen to serve God. The biblical patriarch who had made the statement had chosen God at a time when it was extremely unpopular to do so, at a time when almost everyone else was choosing all kinds of idols. He had courageously chosen God and made a public announcement, heedless of the consequences. It took not only tremendous piety, but also tremendous courage to make such a choice. In the same way, these sidesmen and sideswomen had chosen the service of God at a time when their contemporaries were choosing the idols of materialism, of lechery, of drunkenness, of laziness and self-indulgence, of power, and of egoism. They had chosen to serve God, and by their devotion to duty, their regularity, punctuality, efficiency, and, not least, by this glorious service, they had publicly announced their decision. The heads of Jedi and his colleagues swelled with pride when they heard those statements.

But then, in Jedi's opinion, the preacher had strayed into matters that should not have been his concern. He had gone on to say that the sidesmen and sideswomen should regard themselves as role models, and should ensure that their conduct made them worthy of emulation by both young and old. This was particularly necessary, Rev. Peters said, in this age of decadence, when so many prominent citizens were not only corrupt, but also loose and licentious. So many of them lived in open concubinage or kept their concubines hidden; so many of them corrupted and seduced the very young to whom they were supposed to set a bright example. Was it not common knowledge that scores of apparently respectable, middle-aged men took pleasure in seducing young girls? Did they not even joke about it? Jedi had noticed some of the congregation nodding or even smiling and chuckling in confirmation of what the preacher was saying, and it had made him extremely uneasy, though he did not show it. What business had the preacher to stray into those areas? That was not what they had called him for. He had spoiled an excellent sermon by preaching about things that were not his concern.

Jedi was therefore relieved when the sermon was over. The recession, however, made up for whatever discomfort the sermon had caused. As it was their special day, the sideswomen and sidesmen joined the choir as they recessed from the church. Jedi led them after bowing to the Honorable Minister Distinguished Grand Chief Patron and graciously inviting him to walk by his side in the procession. The Pastor's Warden had to console himself with walking with the minister's lady wife. The other sidesmen and sideswomen followed, but the glory was all Jedi's. He was leading this most elegant and dignified procession with the Honorable Distinguished Minister Grand Chief Patron walking by his side. Glancing to the right and left of the congregation as he strode down the aisle, he held his head high, his shoulders erect, and pushed his burly chest forward.

Jedi was extremely happy as he drove home from church. He traveled along Siaka Stevens Street, through the almost deserted commercial district with its imposing office blocks and shops. Then he turned right into Kroo Town Road, and seemed, all of a sudden, to enter an entirely different world. As usual, Kroo Town Road was bustling with life and although this was a Sunday, one could easily have believed it was a weekday. The shops were closed, but some women had set up little stalls along the roadside from which they sold fruits, vegetables, soap, tinned tomatoes, butter, and so on. The great big market itself on the right hand side was going at full tilt. Jedi found the noise unbearable and couldn't wait to come to the end of the street. He caught sight of Holy Innocents Church, just behind the market, and wondered how its members managed to conduct Sunday morning services with all that noise going on around them. He had always wondered what kind of person became a member of Holy Innocents Church. He glanced down a little street to the right. It ended in an enormous garbage container that was full to overflowing.

As he continued his drive along Kroo Town Road, he noticed the gutter on the left. It seemed to be boiling over with filth, but this had not deterred a young girl from stationing her bread and fried fish stall just a foot away, nor was she short of customers who, having purchased their morning's supplies of her delicacies, stood there and ate them, oblivious of the filth and the stench. Jedi was glad when he turned into Ascension Town Road and then into Hannah Benka-Coker Street which in his opinion, was one of the best streets in Freetown. It was wide and almost entirely free of the potholes that bedeviled most Freetown streets. It had relatively few houses, since to the right were the National Stadium and the Ascension Town cemetery. One did not therefore have that same sense of congestion that characterized Kroo Town Road, for instance.

Jedi continued to enjoy his leisurely drive, his right hand on the wheel, and his left elbow hanging out of the car window. He turned into the equally spacious Brookfields Road, zoomed over the bridge and into Motor Main Road. On reaching Congo Cross, he decided he would take the Aberdeen Ferry Road and make it a long pleasant Sunday drive, instead of proceeding straight to Juba along Wilkinson Road. The Aberdeen Ferry Road took him to Cape Sierra and Lumley Beach, and as he drove along the Cape Road, he admired the majesty of the sky and the greenish-blue sea, and the beauty of the sandy beach that stretched ahead for miles. He looked to the left and saw the equally majestic hills dotted here and there with resplendent modern houses. He looked straight ahead and saw Juba Hill with its own array of beautiful houses, one of them his own: the house he had built out of the sweat of his labor, without borrowing a single cent from anyone. All his! It looked even more beautiful from a distance than it did when one was near it. He breathed a deep sigh of satisfaction, thinking that he had done very well for himself. When he finally turned left into Juba Hill he graciously acknowledged the greetings of friends and neighbors. Having parked the car, he rushed upstairs and went immediately to the balcony to take in once more the panorama of trees, sand, sea, and hills that stretched for miles:. He could think of no more magnificent sight than this. And it was his to enjoy every day. Yes! Life was good!

CHAPTER 4

Jedi's life soon settled down to its usual serene and unruffled pattern. He woke up early in the morning, made his way to the office, executed his official duties in his usual cool and efficient way, chatted and joked with his colleagues, teased the ladies who worked for him, shouted at the messenger, went to church meetings on relevant evenings of the week, and attended church services three times on Sundays. On those evenings when he did not have to attend church meetings, he usually sat on his balcony, a bottle of Heineken beer by his side, half dozing and half gazing at the breathtaking view from his house. Emma King had merely been an unpleasant interlude in his life which he had almost forgotten. Like all successful men, he had dealt with the situation in his usual courageous, forceful and decisive manner.

He had been mildly surprised at how little hue and cry there had been over the disappearance of a schoolgirl. Apparently, Emma and her family were not important enough for anything related to them to be mentioned in the newspapers, even though schoolgirls did not disappear every day in Freetown, and such an incident might therefore have been expected to constitute 'news'. Three days after her 'disappearance,' Emma was mentioned in the daily police report on the radio as having 'absconded' from home. Jedi could not be sure whether it was her family who had decided that she had absconded from home, or whether the police had simply fitted her case into the usual pattern of such announcements. Most young people who went missing were simply reported as having 'absconded' from home. There followed the usual detailed description of Emma's physical features and of her 'haunts,' which in this case included her school and 'Sunday School' gatherings at the Paramount, Brookfields, and other hotels. After about a week, her case was dropped from the police report, most probably to make way for others.

All this worked greatly to Jedi's advantage. It was quite clear that Emma's family and those who had bothered to give the matter a thought did not link her disappearance with murder or foul play. They were not even considering the possibility that she might be dead. Certainly, no one seemed to have linked her disappearance with himself, and that was as it should be, for he had been so discreet that virtually no one knew about his affair with Emma. Once again, he congratulated himself on his foresight and skillful handling of the whole matter.

On a Monday evening, about two weeks after the 'murder,' Jedi was sitting on his verandah with a couple of friends who had come to discuss church matters. Their business having been completed, the three were taking their ease, luxuriously sipping ice-cold beer, gazing at the scene before them, and indulging in parish gossip.

"Don't be deceived by Okiki's solemn demeanor. (Okiki was their forty-five year old curate, assistant to the Vicar.) He also 'eats' whenever he can. I have known him since childhood. We used to play football together."

It was Ethan Spencer, one of Jedi's fellow sidesmen, who contributed the comment.

"A regular womanizer he was. We even shared one or two dames. He dares not look me straight in the eye when he preaches his sermons, because I can see right through him. Ha, ha, ha!"

Jedi and Elkanah Pratt, the other friend, also roared with laughter.

"Someone told me," Elkanah Pratt said, still chuckling, "that when he was being inducted into his last church, one of the parishioners told him, "If you wish to last here, keep your eyes on your Bible and your hands off our women.""

More raucous laughter was booming through the house when Jedi's telephone rang.

Jedi jumped up, excused himself, and went to answer it. His voice conveyed high spirits as he said,

"Hallo, Jedidiah Thomas speaking!"

"You bloody murderer!" It was a cold, hard voice.

Jedi felt as though his head had been struck by a huge boulder. For a moment stars danced before his eyes. His facial features twitched, the hand holding the telephone visibly shook as if he had been suddenly struck by Parkinson's Disease. His legs quaked, his eyes bulged, and his mouth fell open. Trying to grasp the implications of this accusation, he remained silent till the unknown caller repeated it.

"I said you are a bloody murderer."

Realizing that his silence would be taken as an indication of guilt, he managed to blurt out, "Who are you? Whom do you wish to speak to?" then cursed his stupidity. The second question would be considered a weak and ineffectual attempt to play for time because he had announced his name when he picked up the phone.

The cold hard voice went on relentlessly.

"You are a bloody murderer. You are..."

At this point Jedi instinctively slapped down the receiver to stop himself from hearing any more. Sweat broke out over his entire body as he made his way back to his friends in the verandah. They were quick to notice the remarkable change that had come over the normally ebullient Jedi. Elkanah Pratt voiced his concern.

"Is anything the matter? Are you alright, Jedi?"

"I hope you have not received bad news," Ethan put in, similarly concerned about his friend's stunned appearance.

Of course, Jedi could not let them know what had happened. He could not even afford to let them guess that the dramatic change had been brought about by the phone call he had just received. So he said as brightly as he could,

"Oh, I suddenly felt weak. It happens to me sometimes these days, but it will pass. It is nothing."

He hoped this would put an end to the matter, at least to his friends' interest in his health; but he was disappointed. They continued to express their concern, to suggest that he was working too hard, that he should rest, that hypertension was rampant in the country at that moment and he had to be careful and go for medical check-ups, that it was not worth killing himself for the government, that if he collapsed and died, the government would only express sympathy and help arrange a big funeral, that if he died in active service his relations would not even get his due pension. It was not worth Jedi killing himself for that.

Being men of the world, Ethan Spencer and Elkanah Pratt did not for a moment believe that Jedi's altered appearance was caused by sudden weakness. Or if there was weakness at all, it had been caused by that mysterious phone call, and they hoped to probe the mystery out of Jedi by continuing to discuss his health. For his part, sitting in the chair on to which he had slumped, Jedi hardly heard what his two friends were saying. Their voices came to him as from a distance, as from a dream. The reality was that hard, cold voice thundering in his ears, "You are a murderer!"

"Cring! Cring! Cring!" the telephone screamed again, insistently demanding attention. Jedi jumped in his seat and almost shouted his anguish. If his friends had had any doubts that his present state had been caused by the previous telephone call, they had none now. The alarm, horror, and pain on Jedi's face were unmistakable, and beads of sweat had reappeared on his brow.

At first, Jedi ignored the ringing, in the forlorn hope that the caller would give up. But his friends seemed determined that he should answer it.

"Oh these telephones!" Elkanah exclaimed. "They can be such a nuisance. They don't allow people to enjoy peace and quiet."

"And yours is so loud, Jedi," Ethan added. "I think you had better go and take it, Jedi. Don't mind us. It might be someone important; maybe the Vicar calling to talk about the church accounts or something like that. Annoying though it might be, one cannot simply ignore the telephone."

Jedi had no option but to go inside and take the call. In his absence, his friends cast knowing looks at each other. Elkanah's eyes plainly said, "I am sure something nasty is cooking. We shall see." Ethan's expression concurred.

Jedi raised the receiver slowly and deliberately to his ear and said a very faint "yes!"

"You bloody murderer!" yelled the voice. "How dare you slam the phone down on me? You will pay for this. I know you murdered Emma, and I am going to make sure they hang you. Don't think you are too high to be brought to justice. You will beg for mercy before they hang you. You will see."

Before Jedi could react, the caller slammed down the phone. What was this? Jedi thought. Who was this who seemed to know his secret and was determined to torture him? Oh my God! Not hanging! Not death! Jedi's head was swimming as he returned to the verandah. This time his friends were more than concerned about his demeanor. They were truly alarmed. Feeling that he had to be alone to think this matter through, Jedi gave them no time to ask him further questions. He told them he was feeling very ill and needed to lie down for a while.

"Of course," Elkanah said kindly. "We understand. You have obviously been working too hard and need a complete rest. Go to bed at once. And if I were you, I would not even bother to answer the phone again."

"Yes, indeed," added Ethan. "There is nothing more harassing these days than the phone. It is a real scourge. A man goes to bed because he thinks he needs a little rest, and before he has had three winks, "cring". And the worst of it is that once your rest is disturbed, you might find it impossible to go to sleep again."

Elkanah and Ethan left reluctantly. They would have preferred to stay and probe to the bottom of the matter. On their way home they did not hesitate to voice their opinion that the mysterious calls Jedi had received had a lot to do with his sudden indisposition.

"That is why people should try to lead a straightforward life," said Elkanah. "Then they won't be bothered by disturbing phone calls. I can truthfully boast that even if I saw two policemen coming to my door I would not be alarmed because I have absolutely nothing to be afraid or ashamed of."

Far from being asleep or even resting, Jedi was pacing up and down in his bedroom, going through the most agonizing mental torture. Just when he thought he had put the worst crisis of his life solidly behind him and laid a new foundation for his future, it had once more reared its monstrous head and now threatened to destroy him. There was to be no rest for him that day, no rest for him from then on. Up to the time of the first telephone call his future had seemed as promising as it could possibly be. He had laid a new foundation for it and felt he could look forward to a long, glorious, prosperous and distinguished life, respected by the community as a whole and loved and admired by his friends and relations. From now on he could only look forward to harassment, shame, humiliation, exposure, and probably imprisonment and death. Yes, death! That was what the caller had threatened him with. Death! That caller seemed to have enough information, and he sounded cold enough, vicious enough, and determined enough to bring him to the gallows if he wanted to. He was completely in his hands. How was he to prove that he did not murder Emma? Only an autopsy could have determined the cause of her death, and he had disposed of the body. Even if he led the police to where it was, would it not have decomposed so badly by now that a reliable autopsy would not be possible? And would they even be able to find the body after such a long time? Surely, wild animals and vultures would have seen to that. Only the bones would be there; and the bones would not be able to tell anyone what had occurred. How could he establish his innocence? Who would believe him if he told them that the girl had died while he was having sex with her, perhaps from a heart attack, and that he had taken her body and thrown it away in the bush? Would they not rather think that he had killed her to conceal his liaison with her and had then got rid of the body? He realized now what a stupid move it had been to get rid of Emma's body. Only the body could have established that she died of natural causes. Only the body could have established his innocence. He himself had got rid of his only means of salvation. Murder was a hanging matter and the caller seemed to have all the information he needed. All he could look forward to now was death. And not just death, but exposure, humiliation, disgrace. God! This could not really be happening to him. To him of all people. He who had tried to serve his maker honestly and dutifully and discharge his service to the community loyally all his life. It just could not be real!

And who was this caller who was so determined to bring him to the gallows? The voice seemed only vaguely familiar, and much as he pondered over the matter, Jedi still had no clue as to the caller's identity. This deepened his anxiety. If he knew his tormentor he would be in a better position to deal with him. But this individual seemed like a snake that a man knew was hiding somewhere in his house, but had no idea where or how big it was. Yet, he was sure that the moment he lay down and shut his eyes, it would come out and bite him. This was a deadly enemy. For the first time in his life Jedi, who had always felt that every man was master of his fate, that every man could, by his own exertions, decisions and choices direct the course of his destiny, felt that he had no control over his fate. For the first time in his life he felt helpless and trapped.

The next day, he went to work like someone still having a nightmare. The perfunctory greetings he exchanged with his office staff suggested that something was dreadfully wrong with their boss, especially since the normally ebullient Jedi looked sombre and haggard, as though he had not slept all night and was still in the grip of a powerful hangover. When Mrs. Cole went in for her usual instructions and dictation, Jedi gave them as though his mind was not on what he was doing. And there was no wisecrack, no joking, no sharing of office gossip.

There was a planning meeting in his office that morning. The participants-- a Deputy Secretary, an Assistant Secretary, who also served as Secretary for the meeting, and a representative of the professional arm of the ministry-- duly arrived, and the meeting began. To his surprise, Jedi discovered that he could fully concentrate. Yes! This was his element. Work! Once he immersed himself in work he forgot all about his troubles. Perhaps this was the way to deal with this deadly phenomenon that had suddenly appeared in the path of his life. Immerse himself in work! As he debated goals and objectives and strategies and figures with the others, bringing the benefit of his experience and expertise to bear on the issues, he felt once more in control, doing something meaningful in a masterly way to shape the course of events.

For a moment, he took his eyes off the figures on the page before him and glanced at a watercolor painting that hung on the wall opposite. It was only now that he really understood the full significance of the painting and the motives that must have subconsciously impelled him to buy it on one of his trips to America. It was of a cowboy, six feet five inches tall if an inch, with bulging pectorals and biceps, broad-chested and strong-thighed, sitting astride a black bull that similarly exuded strength and power. The bull seemed to be breathing steam from his nostrils, but it was on its knees; that stupendous concentrate of strength, power and fury had been brought to its knees and was about to be tamed by the superior combination of relentless strength, skill and determination of the cowboy. The cowboy's stern eyes, knitted brows, gritted teeth and packed facial muscles suggested not only his determination and sense of purpose, but also his satisfaction at having mastered the black embodiment of brute force. That was control; that was what he, Jedidiah Thomas, exercised daily: directing, shaping and controlling the lives and destinies of thousands.

The meeting went on. He could see in the eyes of his colleagues the respect they had for his professionalism. This was the world in which he excelled, the world of work, where bureaucrats were bringing the benefit of their expertise to bear on the shaping of the nation's destiny. This was the world of meaningful work that that bloody savage, whoever he was, could not possibly comprehend.

The meeting turned out to be one of the most successful that Jedi had ever held. At the end, he and his colleagues relaxed over cups of coffee. Their eyes beamed with satisfaction as they exchanged small banter. The telephone rang. That was no unusual occurrence in Jedi's office. Flushed with satisfaction from the meeting's success, he casually extended his hand and picked up the receiver. His Secretary was at the other end telling him that a Mr. Luke of the Ministry of Trade wanted to speak with him. Jedi knew several Lukes and could not recollect that any of them worked at the Ministry of Trade; but it was possible. Maybe it was one of the new graduates that had just been recruited. As happened all the time, perhaps he wanted to discuss an official problem. Jedi told his Secretary to put him on.

"Mr. Thomas, I want to talk to you about something very important."

It was that voice again. Jedi's heart skipped three beats and his colleagues saw a ghastly expression come over his face.

"Do you hear me, Mr. Thomas?" This time the voice sounded not only mean, but angry, probably because Jedi had not said a word.

"Do you hear me Mr. Thomas? I said I want to talk to you about something very important."

Having glanced at his colleagues, all that Jedi felt he could safely say was, "Yes, I am listening… "

He knew his colleagues would be dying to know who or what had such power to discompose the formidable Jedidiah Thomas.

"I hope you are taking this matter very seriously, Mr. Thomas, because it is very serious. In fact, it is a matter of life and death: *your* life and *your* death."

Jedi's agitation increased when he heard those words. He felt he could not continue the conversation with his colleagues in the room so, doing his utmost to sound normal, he said,

"Excuse me; I am at a meeting right now. Why don't you phone me later or give me your number and I will call you back."

"Do you think I am a fool, Mr. Thomas?" the voice barked; its owner sounded beside himself with fury. "Do you think I am Emma that you can twist around your little finger? Do you really think I will give you my telephone number or tell you where to find me? Listen! *I* shall phone you when and where I want to. Do you understand? Get it into your head that I have it in my power to hang you. From now on I am in control. You will do exactly as I say."

"Thank you, Mr. Luke; you will hear from me shortly."

Though his heart was beating wildly, Jedi put down the receiver as calmly as he could and informed his secretary not to put through any more calls for the time being. He then did his best to regain his composure and brought the meeting formally to a close.

With his colleagues gone, Jedi held his head with his hands and started to ponder this new menace that had come into his life. He must think. What was to be done? Before he could come to any decision the telephone rang again and his secretary told him that that same Mr. Luke was on the line, threatening that both she and her boss would be sorry if she did not put him through immediately, that her boss knew that he had to be put through to him immediately whenever he called him. Jedi had no alternative but to take the call. Until he worked out some kind of strategy, he had to take the calls.

"So, Mr. Thomas, you think you are a big man and that I am a little boy you can treat as you please, eh? You! A bloody murderer! Well, let me tell you. It is the mangy dog that kills the leopard. From now on *I* am the master. You will see. You will lick my anus before you die. I will teach you to screw little girls and kill them. I will make you lick my spittle."

Jedi could only say weakly,

"Who are you? What do you want from me?"

"Aha! You have as good as admitted your guilt? I will tell you who I am. I am the one who will put the rope around your neck. As for what I want from you, I shall phone you later and give you your instructions. All in good time! And remember! I am now the master. So don't you dare slam the phone down on me again or refuse to take the call if you value your life. Bye bye."

By this time, Jedi was shaking all over and dripping with sweat even though his office was air-conditioned. It was now obvious to him that he had fallen into the clutches of a vicious individual determined to destroy him. O God! What had he done to deserve being in the power of someone like that, someone who used the kind of vulgar language he had just heard? Why had he been so stupid? Why had he not merely reported Emma's death? His torturer sounded as though he had enough information to hang him. If that was the case, he was as good as dead. Another thought occurred to Jedi at this point. Why had the caller not gone straight to the police with the damning information so that they could arrest him? Maybe he was only interested in blackmail. *He could use it to torture and humiliate me for as long as he pleases,* Jedi thought wretchedly.

His mind was such a melee of agonizing thoughts that he did not see how he could continue with work that day. He told his secretary that he was feeling indisposed again, left the office, went home, and went straight to bed. For an hour or so he continued to agonize over his situation until his thoughts were once again rudely interrupted by the ringing of the telephone.

Oh God! For a moment, Jedi considered simply refusing to answer it. But he remembered the voice's fury and threats the last time he had slammed the phone down, so, ever so slowly, he reached out, gingerly picked up the phone, and after about several seconds, put it to his ear.

"Yes!"

"Is that the murderer speaking?" This time the voice was lower but still bold. Jedi now thought that he had given in too easily in the past. He had behaved as though he were guilty, although he knew of no definite evidence the caller had against him. At least, he should put on a veneer of innocence. So he shouted into the receiver.

"Who are you, and why do you keep calling me a murderer?"

"Don't you dare shout at me, Mr. Thomas! Murderer! Don't you dare shout at me. I have already told you who I am. I am the one who is going to put the rope around your neck. You ask me why I call you a murderer, as though you don't know why. You killed your juvie girl friend, Emma, and hid her body. That is why I call you a murderer."

"That is a bloody lie!"

"Stupid man! Stupid man! You think I would make such serious allegations if I did not have enough evidence? You think no one saw you with Emma that night? Well, get ready to piss in your trousers. I know that Emma visited you that evening because I saw her enter your house. And she never came out again alive. I saw you bringing her body into your garage in a rice bag and dumping it into the trunk of your car. And I saw you drive out with it in that terrible storm. You know that what I am saying is true. I shall announce it to the whole world unless you do as I say."

Jedi felt weak at the knees. There was no doubt now that the caller had information that he had imagined that no one else had. The feeling of utter helplessness once more overwhelmed him.

"So what do you want from me?"

"Right. I am glad you now know who is master. Meet me at King Jimmy tonight at twelve midnight. Go down the steps leading to the wharf from Wallace Johnson Street. Then go into the market building. I shall be waiting for you there. Be sure to come alone or I shall have nothing more to do with you. I shall go straight to the police and give them all the information I have. Those are your instructions for now. I shall give you more when I see you tonight. No tricks."

With that, the caller slammed down the phone.

Jedi was somewhat relieved, for it was clear that the caller did not desire his death. At least, not for now. Maybe there was the possibility of some kind of negotiation. For the first time since the calls started, that feeling of being under sentence of death lightened a little. Tonight he would find out the caller's identity and what he wanted from him. But dare he go alone to King Jimmy wharf in the middle of the night? He knew that the place was the haunt of all kinds of cutthroats and drug addicts. Suppose he found himself surrounded by a whole crowd of thugs? What would he do? Was it wise to go alone? Perhaps he should ask a friend to accompany him. But that would mean giving some explanation to the friend, and he could not do that. Besides, the voice had ordered him to go alone, and, for good or ill, he had to obey. Yes that voice was surely his master now. That voice...Where had he heard it before? The question nagged, but he could find no answer.

And so at a quarter to twelve that night, Jedi left his house and made his way by car to King Jimmy Wharf. He knew that the King Jimmy area was not the kind of locality that would be frequented by decent, law-abiding citizens at that time of night. He began to wonder whether the choice of rendezvous was not a deliberate insult. Suppose someone he knew saw him about to descend the steps leading to that disreputable wharf at that time of night? He would not be able to live down the disgrace. He would have to make himself unrecognizable; in fact, as much like a thug as possible.

Jedi therefore wore a very old pair of blue jeans, a pair of black tennis shoes that he had not worn for ages, his oldest brown shirt, a black vinyl windcheater, and a black cloth 'facing' cap which he pulled down well over his eyes. He parked his car just outside the police headquarters at George

Street where he was sure it would be safe, and then walked the half a mile or so to King Jimmy. The streets were almost deserted at that hour, for this was the official and commercial area where very few people actually lived, although there were a number of seedy nightclubs in the vicinity with the usual stragglers loitering outside. As he was about to start descending the steps leading to the wharf, he saw two dubious looking male characters hanging around the entrance. They were obviously up to no good, and each gave him a rather threatening look as he started his descent. At first, he felt sure that they could not be related to the voice because the latter had clearly instructed him to go inside the market building. But it immediately occurred to him that they might be lookouts. It thus dawned on him for the first time that he might be dealing, not just with one individual, but with a whole conspiracy of thugs. If that was the case, then his prospects were bleak indeed. The more people who knew his secret, the more likely it was to become public. Jedi decided that it was best to ignore the two thugs and proceed down the steps, but he realized that his knees were wobbly and he had begun to sweat. That was bad. He should certainly not appear weak in the presence of his tormentor. Summoning as much courage as he could in the circumstances, he walked into the market building.

It was in darkness and almost deserted but for two shapes that he saw huddled and writhing on one of the tables in one corner. It was too dark for Jedi to make out their sex, but the low moans and gasps emanating from them left him in no doubt as to what they were up to. He once again realized how degrading it was that he should have been brought to such a place at this time of night.

"Good evening, Mr. Thomas," a low voice called out from the left hand corner.

Ah! So this was his tormentor. He could not yet make out the face, but the form suggested a powerfully built young male about six feet tall. Without saying a word, Jedi approached him and looked into the face of... Yes! It was the young man Emma had been with when he first met her at that 'Sunday School'. No wonder there had been something familiar about the voice!

Jedi's first reaction was one of fierce indignation that he had been terrorized and manipulated by an insignificant scumbag who was no more than twenty or so. Completely oblivious of his surroundings, Jedi thundered at him,

"How dare you bring me to such a place at this time of night? How dare you threaten me with your stupid calls? I have the good mind to thrash you within an inch of your worthless life."

The young man's mouth dropped open in surprise and remained so for a few seconds. Then he let out a peal of laughter.

"You still don't understand, Mr. Thomas. You still think that you are in control, that I am a kind of worm, and that your position in society will make you get away with murder. Well, I have told you; it is the mangy dog that kills the leopard. I have information that can hang you, and I will use it to hang you unless you learn to respect me as your master and take my orders."

He had raised his voice, as bullies do, and realizing the danger, Jedi begged him to lower his voice. This matter was between the two of them, he said. At this, the young man smiled, saying he always knew that Jedi was an intelligent man who would see reason.

******

Yes, the young man who had succeeded in reducing Jedi to a position of bootlicking servitude was none other than Emma King's boyfriend, Abdul Sanusi. He was twenty-two years old and had no regular employment. His family had sent him to school but, being completely uninterested in education, he had dropped out of secondary school in the second form. He looked around him and saw a lot of men and women, Sierra Leoneans as well as non-Sierra Leoneans, flourishing like proverbial green bay trees although they had little or no education, while a number of highly educated men and women seemed to be living on the verge of poverty. He therefore concluded that one did not need education to succeed in life and decided that he would make his fortune by whatever means presented itself. He naturally gravitated towards other boys like himself, who moved in gangs, and he learned the language and the skills of the street. He knew that he was good-looking and hoped that one day he would be able to attach himself to some wealthy man or woman, maybe some tourist, who would help make his fortune. In the meantime, as he grew older, he began to hang around bars, cinemas, night-clubs and hotels, befriending the ladies of pleasure who frequented them. He served some of them well as protector and pimp, and they became fond of him. Some even lusted after him, which was not surprising. In truth, Abdul was a remarkably handsome young man: well-built, and at six foot five one of the tallest young men in the city. He also possessed a powerful chest and broad shoulders, a slim waist, bulging biceps and hair that curled like an Arab's. This fortunate combination of physical qualities attracted women and girls to him in droves, and he had already discovered that he could make quite a comfortable living off them.

As a frequenter of hotels, Abdul also went to the 'Sunday Schools' held at the hotels and preyed on the young girls there. That was how he met Emma King. In no time, Emma doted on him and was prepared to do anything for him. She was even reputed to have said that if it were necessary to kill for him she was quite prepared to do so. Abdul had known about Emma's liaison with Jedi, but pimp and gigolo that he was, he was used to having girl friends who performed sexual services for other men. In fact, he saw these girls almost as his personal resources to be exploited on the market. He always managed to get the lion's share of their takings from their doting 'sugar daddies', so most of what Emma received from Jedi found itself into Abdul's pockets and helped pay for an extravagant lifestyle and flamboyant clothes.

On a Sunday, one month before her death, as they relaxed in Abdul's room before setting out for 'Sunday School,' Emma had informed him that she had not seen her period. To her great dismay, Abdul fumed and thundered and, using the harsh gutter language of street boys, threatened to put a knife to her throat if she dared mention his name in connection with any pregnancy. Then he remembered Jedi whom he had long seen as a kind of insurance policy, so after his initial reaction, his attitude softened and he said Emma should tell Jedi that *he* was the father and get him to finance an abortion. Emma agreed readily enough. Abdul was the man of her heart and Jedi merely a supplier of cash. She was not by any means in love with him, and sometimes even ridiculed him in conversations with her friends.

That was how Emma came to visit Jedi's house on that fateful day. What Jedi did not know was that she had not gone alone. Suspecting that Jedi might want to wriggle out of the difficult situation of being responsible for a schoolgirl's pregnancy, Abdul wanted to be close at hand in case it became necessary to beat up or blackmail him into acquiescence. He had arranged with Emma that he would keep out of sight as she entered Jedi's house, but that he would hang around the area, ready to break in and accost her 'sugar daddy' if the situation required it. When Emma failed to emerge after several hours inside, Abdul became not only concerned, but also suspicious. He scaled Jedi's wall without much difficulty and crouched behind a tree, vowing to lie in wait, all night if necessary, until he saw Emma emerge from the house.

But Emma never appeared. Instead, the terrific storm began. Abdul decided that he stood a much better chance of surviving its onslaught if he hid under the eaves of Jedi's house than if he ventured out into the street and tried to make his way home. It was while he was in this position that he had heard sounds and, by peeping through a breeze block in the garage wall, saw Jedi struggling into his garage with a rice bag which obviously contained something extremely heavy. He saw Jedi load the bag into the trunk of his car and drive out into the rain. Though Abdul did not actually see Emma's body, the shape of the bag strongly suggested the contours of a human body. And where was Emma? She had not left the house, and she had not intended to stay the night with Jedi. In any case, why would Jedi leave her alone in the dead of night, and why would he go out when the most terrible storm to hit Freetown in decades was raging? Abdul was absolutely sure that Jedi had killed Emma and was going to dispose of her body. Since he could not follow him, he remained in his hiding place until Jedi returned, and decided to stay until the morning to see whether Emma would finally emerge. But as he had expected, that did not happen. When it was later revealed that the girl was missing, that confirmed Abdul's suspicions.

His first reaction was outrage. It was not due to any kind of feeling that the girl he loved had been murdered. Abdul did not love Emma. He had merely exploited her for cash. The outrage was due, rather, to his disgust that a man, who pretended to be so respectable, had committed such a heinous crime. No doubt, Mr. Thomas thought that his position would enable him to get away with it. In that case, it was up to him, Abdul, to ensure that he did not. His problem was this. What should he do? At first he thought of going to the police with his story, but on second thoughts, he decided on a different course of action; the police were thoroughly unreliable, inefficient, and corrupt. Even if they arrested Jedi, he would probably be able to bribe his way out of trouble, especially as he, Abdul, did not know where Jedi had buried the body. It would be difficult for a charge to stick if there was no body. Then only the police would reap any benefit from the information he had obtained. With Emma dead, one of his sources of income had dried up, so he should not let slip this opportunity to make money and let it pass into the hands of the police. In fact, if he was smart, Emma dead would be much more profitable to him than Emma alive. He could milk Jedi for all he was worth.

Abdul virtually danced with glee when the full implications of the course he was about to embark on dawned on him. By blackmailing Mr. Thomas he would not only be ensuring his own financial security, he would also be in a position to enjoy the man's suffering and misery. The prospect of reducing such a pompous individual to misery and possible poverty thrilled his very soul. Besides, blackmailing Mr. Thomas would give him a satisfying feeling of power and superiority for a change. In fact, Abdul decided, he would first reduce him to abject submission and penury and, when he had milked him dry, surrender him to the police. He would play with him the way a cat played with an injured mouse that he was going to kill anyway. He would play him for all he was worth and then finally kill him. Yes! This was power.

******

Abdul looked at the scruffy individual standing in front of him, still pretending to be superior to him. Why, he thought, had he ever regarded this fool as a big man? As his six- foot-five-inch frame towered above Jedi, the latter seemed to shrink. Why did he and Emma ever think that this rat was anything that anyone should respect? He could not have been more disgusted had he stepped accidentally on feces. His disgust registered in the tone he now adopted.

"Now here are your instructions, ekuru dog!"

"What do you mean...?" Jedi started indignantly. He was going to say more, but Abdul loudly and peremptorily cut him off in such a way that there was no doubt in either's mind as to who was master.

"Shut your stinking mouth. Do you hear me? Don't you dare speak when I am speaking. One more word from you without my permission and I am off to the police. It will all come out and everything will be over."

Jedi recalled that they were not alone in the building; there were at least two other disreputable people there who would not hesitate to exploit the situation if they overheard what Abdul was saying. He dared not say another word, so he made imploring gestures with his hands, his head, and his entire body, begging Abdul to be quiet. The gestures reinforced his servility, which did not fail to register with the merciless Abdul.

"You know that I am now your master and I can make them hang you whenever I feel like it. You will not say anything, unless I tell you to, and you will do exactly as I say. The price for my silence is six hundred thousand leones. You will meet me at the entrance of the City Hotel tomorrow at half past twelve exactly and hand over the money. Understand?"

Jedi felt he had been given permission to speak, so he blurted out,

"Six hundred thousand leones! Where do you expect me get it?"

"How you get it is none of my business," Abdul said coldly. "Mortgage your house or sell your mother or whatever. Just turn up at the City Hotel tomorrow at half past twelve with six hundred thousand leones. I know you have it. And remember, no tricks! If I see you even winking to anyone, the word will be out, and you will face the consequences."

"Okay, okay I shall bring you a cheque."

Abdul gave such a shout of scornful laughter that Jedi almost jumped out of his skin.

"So you still take me for a fool, Mr. Thomas. You think I will take a cheque from you, a cheque that can later be traced or even cancelled? The deal is over."

To Jedi's horror, Abdul started walking out of the building. Had he been thinking clearly, he might have called Abdul's bluff, but the young man's brazenness and his own guilt had reduced him to a tattered bundle of nerves. Feeling as terrified as a small antelope about to be swallowed by a boa constrictor and strangled in its deadly embrace, Jedi actually ran after Abdul, fell down and clutched his feet.

"All right, all right!" he pleaded. "I beg! I will do as you say. I will bring the six hundred thousand leones in cash, and I will come alone."

"You better do that, if you know what is good for you" Abdul answered. He extricated his foot with a kick and disappeared into the darkness.

CHAPTER 5

The City hotel was located in the heart of Freetown, in the midst of the commercial and bureaucratic district. It was a seedy run-down establishment that could by no means compete with the more modern, more luxurious hotels along the beach. However, it had some historical and therefore touristic value. It had been the only hotel in Freetown in the colonial era, and the opening scene of the English writer Graham Greene's *Heart of the Matter* took place on its balcony. Also, it was the best place to go for the latest news in town, because there were always lots of civil servants and business people there. The proprietor was a likeable and popular European man.

At the time of day that Abdul specified, the City Hotel was usually full of government functionaries, all eager to down a few pints of beer and catch the latest gossip, so it surprised no one when Jedidiah Thomas showed up.

Jedi could not recollect how he had managed to get home the previous night after his rendezvous with Abdul. His mind had been in a complete whirl. He must have steered his car like a robot, or his car must have known the way home and steered itself, for he was quite sure that he had been in no position to concentrate on his driving. He could not remember how he took the turns or whether he stopped at the intersections. When he got home he poured himself a stiff whisky and considered his options. His first thought was to renege on the commitment he had made to Abdul: absolutely refuse to give him a cent. Why should this parasite, who had probably not done an honest day's work in his whole life, lay claim to such a substantial proportion of his hard-earned money? If there was one group of people that the upright Jedi hated, it was those lazy folks who refused to work and thought they could live off the substance of others. So far he had been resolute that such people should have none of his resources. They deserved to be stamped out of society. Abdul was a criminal who deserved to be behind bars. He should really go to the police and report that he was being blackmailed. The maximum penalty for blackmail was life imprisonment. That was what Abdul would get. He had enough clout to ensure that Abdul got the maximum punishment.

As such thoughts roamed in his mind, Jedi began to feel more confident. He even began to imagine the look on Abdul's face when, instead of being met by a servile Jedi and being handed an envelope containing six hundred thousand leones, he was grabbed by two stalwart policemen, whacked on his head with murderous truncheons, and led to jail in handcuffs. That was what he deserved. But then the thought of the police and of jail brought Jedi back to reality. Once the police were brought into the matter he would be finished. He knew how corrupt policemen were. Even if he were the innocent party, they would try to get as much out of him as possible before doing anything about the case. And Abdul would make certain that he, Jedi, was not regarded as the offended party. During their rendezvous at King Jimmy, he had as good as confessed everything, and, faced with the prospect of life imprisonment, Abdul would divulge all he knew. There were probably even witnesses. It could well be that those two reprobates who had been engaged in some shady activity in a corner of the market had been stationed there by Abdul. No! He could not take the risk of going to the police.

It then occurred to Jedi that he could get Roger Neal, his lawyer friend, to threaten Abdul: threaten him with arrest, conviction and life imprisonment. But then, was Abdul the type that would succumb to threats of any kind? Did he not know that he was on to a good thing from which no threats would divert him? Did he not know that it was he who was in the position of making the ultimate threat, the threat of the gallows? Besides, even if Abdul was the kind to succumb to threats, could Jedi really bring himself to confide in his lawyer friend? He would have to explain why he was being blackmailed. That meant that he would have to tell the lawyer about Emma. Roger Neal would surely advise him to go to the police. It was the step he had wanted to avoid by going to a lawyer. Even if he did not advise him to go to the police, Jedi knew that Roger would take a very dim view of his shady activities and when Jedi left his office, would probably wash his hands in disgust or spit out his contempt. No! He could not go to Roger Neal.

The more Jedi considered his options, the more he realized that he had no alternative but to do as Abdul wanted. Yes! That Abdul had him firmly in his grip. Abdul had the power of life and death over him. How had he, a very senior civil servant, a highly educated man, a pillar of the community, a leader of his church, come to be the victim of a mean, illiterate, penniless, parasite like Abdul? Well, he would have to do what had to be done. He would let Abdul have the money tomorrow, but he would be very firm and tell him that there was nothing more where that came from. Six hundred thousand leones was a lot of money, but if that was the price he had to pay for his freedom and peace of mind, it would be well worth it. He had to be free from the terror of the last two days.

When Jedi went to the bank the following day and presented his cheque for six hundred thousand leones, the cashier was flabbergasted. It was quite some time since anyone had tried to withdraw such a large sum of money in cash. But she knew Jedi had at least that amount of money in his account, so she was sure there was nothing fishy about the transaction. Jedi collected his money, put it in a bulky envelope, and made his way to the City Hotel. Abdul had said that they should meet in the foyer, but Jedi did not want anyone he knew to see him meeting an obviously disreputable fellow like Abdul. So having bought a beer and exchanged some banter with acquaintances in the foyer, Jedi made his way out on to the verandah to await Abdul's arrival. He had expected that Abdul, who was quite clearly greedy for the money, would be waiting for him, but Jedi now realized that it was customary for the master to make the servant wait. Abdul was absolutely sure that he was now master, so he would make Jedi wait.

After a while, he saw Abdul approaching. He was quite decently dressed. In fact, had Jedi not known more about him, he would have thought that, like so many of the people there, Abdul was a civil servant or an employee of one of the companies. With his imposing build and good looks, he was clearly someone most people would not mind being seen with. Knowing what Abdul was doing to him, however, Jedi put on his ugliest expression, but to his surprise, Abdul extended a hand and greeted him as affably, as if they were close friends of long standing. No one would ever have suspected that the most sordid transaction was about to take place between them. Instead of asking him for the money or suggesting that they sit down together at a table and "do business," Abdul left him and went into the foyer where he proceeded to greet most people there with similar affability and bonhomie. And they, too, were profuse in their greetings.

What was this boy about? Jedi wondered. Was he trying to show that he, too, had contacts, or that, as far as many other people were concerned, he was not a thug? Or was he merely trying to divert suspicion from the activity that he and Jedi were soon to engage in? Or maybe these were people with whom he had done business before. These days there were so many men going about as if butter wouldn't melt in their mouths, pretending to be loyal husbands and good churchmen when, in actual fact, they all had girl friends, even 'juvies' on the side. At least, *he* was not married. And why had Abdul not asked him directly for the money? Was he trying to suggest that he was not all that anxious? After all, he was the master and could take his time. You had to hand it to this young man; for sheer bloody cheek and gall he would be hard to beat.

Eventually, Abdul returned to the verandah, put his arm companionably around Jedi's shoulder and steered him outside to a shed nearby where hardly anyone would see them. His demeanor changed immediately. The smile disappeared and it was the stern face of a judge that now glared down at Jedi and held out his hand,

"The money."

If during the last few minutes Jedi had allowed himself to think that Abdul would be gentle with him, he now realized that he was completely mistaken.

"Here it is," he answered hurriedly and humbly.

He handed over the brown parcel in which he had wrapped the white envelope containing the money. Abdul extracted the money, which was in thousand leone notes, quickly and expertly checked to see that there were really six hundred of them, and returned them to the envelope.

"Well, Mr. Thomas," he said with a broad smile, "I can see you are a man who knows how to do business."

"I had to borrow from people to make up the amount, so please don't bother asking me for more." Jedi told him, "I have no more money to give you."

"Of course, of course! I do realize that," Abdul replied. "Do you think I am that wicked? My price was six hundred thousand and you have obeyed my instructions and paid it. I can see that you are a true churchman, a real man of God. From now on consider yourself a free man. Go on and enjoy your life. It's been great doing business with you. Good bye."

And Abdul went back inside to fraternize with his numerous acquaintances.

Jedi breathed a tremendous sigh of relief. Well, thank God that was over. It was amazing how well things had turned out in the end. A few hours before he was shaking with trepidation, thinking he was in the clutches of some relentless monster. Now he was free. It had cost him a lot of money, but he could afford it. In the end, Abdul had turned out to be quite a reliable, even decent negotiator. Jedi would never forget the smile on the young man's face after he finished counting the money and as he said, "Now you can go on with your life, Mr. Thomas." A foreman of the jury pronouncing the verdict of "not guilty" to a prisoner accused of murder could not have sounded more pleasing to the ears.

It was always good to be straightforward. He had agreed to let Abdul have the six hundred thousand leones and he had brought and given it to him, down to the last leone. Straightforwardness was one of the values his mother had taught him: if you are straightforward with people, she always said, they will be straightforward with you. She had trained him in the way he should go and as an adult he had not departed from it.

The sun was blazing down from a cloudless blue sky, and yet it was not uncomfortably hot, for there was a slight breeze wafting in from the sea. As Jedi walked back to his office, he heard birds singing and found himself whistling, too. He felt an extraordinary fellowship with the birds and tried to follow their progress as they glided effortlessly in the air. He noticed the flowers that had been planted in front of one of the commercial houses. Strange that he had never noticed them before. They were bright yellow, blue and red; so beautiful. Yes! It was good to be alive. Some of the acquaintances he met on the way might have been mildly surprised by the affability with which he greeted them that day, even stopping to exchange good-natured chit-chat with them which was most unusual.

That was in February. Two months later, Jedi decided to celebrate his fiftieth birthday in grand style. He planned a lavish party to which his closest friends and relations would be invited. He had indeed been getting on with his life and had almost forgotten about Emma and the vicious young man who had made him pay for his escapade. His work at the ministry proceeded smoothly and he continued to discharge his duties at his church with his usual efficiency. There was no diminution in the regard and esteem in which he was held. His birthday party would be a celebration of his successful life and career.

It took place on the last Saturday in April. That evening, Jedi paused to contemplate the lavish preparations he had made. He had rented special chairs from the town hall because there would be about eighty people present. Some of the chairs had been arranged upstairs on both sides of the L shaped balcony, some on the downstairs verandah, and some on three sides of the enormous lounge. On the fourth side, the young but experienced DJ was already busy with his state-of-the-art stereophonic sound system, from which dance music was already blaring. The upstairs and downstairs ceilings were festooned with garlands and balloons, and the birthday feast specially prepared by one of the most expensive caterers in town was ready to be served: jollof rice and a delicious chicken, pork, and beef stew to go with it; a whole roast pig holding a large red tomato in its mouth; a whole baked barracuda; and a salad with baked beans, onions, eggs and salmon, all of which would amount to several thousand calories per helping. There were also sausage rolls, fried plantains, fried liver, peppered steak as well as other delicacies to tempt every palate.

Jedi knew that at such parties, people liked to drink excessively at the host's expense, so he had decided to show that he could afford any drink his guests might wish for and would not be parsimonious. Apart from several bottles of whisky, rum, gin, and brandy, he had bought several crates of beer, stout, and 'soft' drinks, and, since his freezer could not take that many bottles, he had put some of them on ice in two of his three bathtubs. He knew that the success of any party depended on the guests having what they wanted when they wanted it, so he had drafted Juldeh into service with two messengers from his office. All three of them were already there, resplendent in their white uniforms and with brilliantly white towels draped over their arms. They had been carefully instructed about the proper way of handing out, pouring out or mixing drinks. Jedi had asked three female cousins to help out with serving the food when the time came. As he surveyed the scene he saw with great pleasure that all was exactly as it ought to be. No one would say that Jedidiah Thomas did not know how to throw a party. Yes! Here, he was master.

An hour and a half later, at about half past ten, almost all of the guests had arrived. Jedi had invited the top echelons of society. There were quite a few permanent secretaries and deputy secretaries, some lawyers, physicians, and college professors, engineers, architects and a few members of his church including the irrepressible Ethan Spencer and Elkanah Pratt, even a couple of cabinet ministers and one or two members of parliament. The dance area in the lounge downstairs, was always crowded because the DJ certainly knew the kind of music that would get this particular group of people on their feet and keep them dancing. Juldeh and the two office messengers kept the drinks flowing. *This is a wonderful party*, Jedi thought happily, *even if I say so myself.*

"So, how does it feel to be fifty?" asked Ethan Spencer when he was able to catch Jedi alone for a moment.

"Oh, I don't feel fifty at all," Jedi replied with a hearty laugh. "Maybe life really begins at fifty, instead of forty, as they say. I feel as if I could walk the three and half miles to Lumley Beach and back without feeling it at all."

"I am sure you would too, "replied Ethan. "You seem to be in much better shape these days:better than a lot of young men of twenty-five, ha! ha! ha!"

Then, "Cring cring! Cring cring! Cring cring! Cring cring…" screamed the telephone.

"Excuse me, Ethan, let me take that call," Jedi said turning to the telephone hooked on to the back wall of the lounge near where they were standing. He was all geniality and smiles as he picked up the receiver.

"Hello! Jedi here! What can I do you for on this beautiful evening?"

"Hello, Mr. murderer!"

Jedi almost dropped the receiver. His hand, indeed his whole body visibly shook. Words froze on his lips and his face, which a moment ago had been radiant ebony, had turned a ghastly gray. Sweat bathed his entire body all at once and started soaking through his shirt. And what was that fluid slowly trickling down his right leg?

"Mr. girl murderer, didn't you hear me? I said hello. Or do you think I do not deserve a reply? I can hear music and laughter in the background. So you are having a party and did not think I was good enough to be invited to meet all your 'aristo' friends. What are you celebrating, Emma's death? Have you told your friends that you murdered a young girl, or do you want me to come over and tell them for you? I am willing to oblige…"

By this time Jedi had summoned enough presence of mind to put down the receiver without saying a word. But as he moved away from the phone he was far from the happy, ebullient person he had been a moment before. He was sure that the sweat and expression on his face were noticeable and he could feel that line of liquid flowing down his right leg. Ethan Spencer gave him a rather quizzical look as he dashed up the stairs to change his trousers, so he quickly muttered "wrong number." and fled.

In the privacy of his bedroom Jedi had time to think. So that bastard was after him again. What kind of devil was he? Hadn't he assured Jedi that everything was over, that he was free and would be allowed to get on with his life? And just when he felt really free, when he had all but forgotten about Emma and murder and being blackmailed, the treacherous dog had come back to hound him. He had been living in a fool's paradise. And to think that Abdul had chosen to come back into his life and torture him on the very day that he was celebrating his successful life with his closest and most esteemed friends and relations! This vicious brute who did not know anything about the decencies of civilized life, who could probably not spell 'success' even if he knew what it meant! To think that he was at his mercy! If Abdul had the temerity to come back into his life after he had got his six hundred thousand leones and had assured him that he was free, would he ever stop? Would he not go on until he had reduced him to penury, disgraced him or contrived his death on the gallows? At the thought of what might lie ahead Jedi groaned, wishing that he could suddenly disappear. At least he would be out of Abdul's reach.

He put on as brave a face as he could as he went to rejoin his guests. Not many of the people busy enjoying themselves paid any attention to him; but he could not avoid Ethan Spencer who had positioned himself so that he could see Jedi's face as he came down the stairs. He went up to Jedi, his own face exuding sympathy and concern.

"I hope nothing is wrong," he said. "You looked ill again as you went upstairs."

"Oh, it's nothing," Jedi replied. "What with the crowd and the dancing I had started to sweat and decided to go up and change."

Very clever, thought Ethan, though he said nothing out loud. *"Jedi has wriggled out of it well, but that telephone call rattled him, just like the one he had the last time Elkanah and I were here. I bet there is something nasty going on and I intend to get to the bottom of it.*

For his part, Jedi started mingling with his guests once more. But no sooner did he start doing so than the telephone rang again loudly, relentlessly, and insistently, demanding to be answered. Jedi let it ring, not because he thought it was the wisest thing to do, but because he was terrified of what he might hear if he picked it up. If Abdul's intention was to reduce him to a nervous wreck, he was well on the way to success.

Juldeh heard the phone ring and realized that his master was not going to answer it. Assuming that it was one of his duties at a party like this, he unhooked the receiver and said, "Hello, this..."

"You dirty thing!" shouted the voice at the other end. "How dare you slam down the phone on me again? Have I not told you not to do that anymore?"

Anyone paying attention to Juldeh, as Ethan Spencer was, would have realized that he was completely taken aback by what he heard coming from the other end, for his jaw dropped. Indeed, Juldeh had never heard such anger, such hatred, and such vulgarity expressed over the phone in his life.

"Eh eh!" he said. "What is this? This is Mr. Thomas's house and I am his steward. Are you sure you have got the right number? "

"Well, steward," said the voice, "just tell your Mr. Thomas that someone wants to talk to him about something very important, and do it now!"

"Yes, sir!" Juldeh answered like a new recruit before a sergeant-major. He then stepped up to Jedi and said loudly enough for everyone to hear,

"Boss, the person on the line says he has to talk to you about something very important, sir."

Jedi had no alternative but to go and pick up the receiver. He was aware of a number of curious eyes looking on and knew he had to be careful about what he said.

"Hello!"

"Mr. Thomas, you are a dirty old man and a bloody murderer," the voice roared. "I am going to tell the whole world that you are a juvie lover and a murderer and I am going to make them hang you!"

Jedi felt himself shaking as he heard those terrible words again, but he realized that Ethan Spencer, Elkanah Pratt, and a few others were watching him and resolved to remain as composed as was possible in the circumstances.

"Yes," he said, "what do you want me to do now?"

"I want your life, Mr. Thomas, murderer."

Jedi felt as if his whole frame was dissolving; and that that trickle of liquid might start flowing down his leg again. However, he managed to maintain his outward composure.

"I thought we had settled all this," he said in as low a tone as he could contrive.

"Settled all this?" the voice shouted in apparent disbelief. "Ha, ha, ha, ha, ha."

To Jedi the raucous laughter sounded like the tolling of a bell.

"You must be stupid," the voice sneered. "I thought you were an intelligent man. Did you really think that six hundred thousand leones could buy a life? It is a life we are talking about here, man. In fact, we are talking about two lives: Emma's life, and your life. Maybe a man in your position doesn't think that the life of a girl like Emma is worth much, but what about your own life? How much do you think your life is worth, Mr. Murderer?"

At this point Jedi felt that if he heard anymore he would collapse there and then. He said in his most polished English accent,

"As you can hear, I am entertaining friends, so I cannot discuss anything in detail now. Please call me tomorrow and we can have a nice chat about it."

"Don't you dare slam down the phone on me. *I* will tell you when this conversation is over. Remember; I am the master now."

But Jedi really had to put down the phone and rejoin his guests.

"Oh these phones!" one guest remarked. "Fancy harassing someone on a night like this. Sometimes I think the telephone is more of a curse than a blessing…"

"Cring!!!!!!!!!!!!!" the telephone screamed again.

Juldeh looked at his master, not sure what to do. Jedi was not sure what to do either, but one of his guests came to the rescue with an excellent suggestion.

"Just take it off the hook for the rest of the evening."

Everyone agreed that it was a splendid idea and Jedi took the advice. His guests soon forgot the phone calls and went on to enjoy the rest of the splendid party as if nothing had happened. Jedi, however, was never quite the same that night. He had been badly shaken and knew that Abdul would take revenge on him for disconnecting the phone; he was a vicious young man.

Jedi did not know how he got through the rest of the party. He had to be reminded by one of his cousins that it was high time the food was served. He could not remember anything that was said when the toasts were being proposed; he was sure that his own speech thanking everyone was rambling, incoherent rubbish. When asked to cut the cake he slashed it viciously from end to end instead of making an exquisite cut from the center to the perimeter. The party became easily the worst birthday celebration he had ever had. As his friends expressed their good wishes, the terms "happy birthday" and "many happy returns of the day," sounded full of irony.

The next day was Sunday, and normally Jedi would have gone to church, for as the People's Warden, he was therefore expected to attend both morning services. Except on those rare occasions when he was ill he did this unfailingly. That Sunday, however, he decided that he was in no mood for church, and telephoned the Vicar's Warden to make his excuses. Strangely, it did not occur to the God-fearing Jedi that, of all Sundays, this was the one on which he needed to pray for deliverance from a deadly enemy. Juldeh did not normally work on Sundays, but Jedi had asked him to come in so he could clean up after the party. He could already hear him downstairs going about his business in his usual efficient way.

After his bath, Jedi put on underpants and a dressing gown and sat on the balcony to clear his head and think. It was an extremely beautiful and peaceful morning, and therefore conducive to thinking. The sun was already climbing the sky and the Atlantic Ocean looked simply magnificent. The three-mile stretch of sand that was Lumley Beach seemed to sparkle in the distance. He could see some early bathers already taking advantage of the calm waters to go for a morning swim. This must be one of the most beautiful pieces of real estate on God's earth and part of it was Jedi's to enjoy. He had been enjoying it and would certainly have continued to enjoy it but for this demon that had come into his life. He wondered what Abdul's next move would be. One thing was certain: he would do something terrible. Why had he called him on the night of his birthday? It was surely because he wished to extort more money from him. And now that he was enraged because Jedi had hung up on him, he would probably do something even more devastating. Had he known that he was going to have a birthday party? Jedi wondered. He had probably been stalking him during the last two months when he thought he was safe, watching his every move or making enquiries about him and his activities, and he had probably chosen this particular occasion to strike because he knew that Jedi would be at his happiest and would be surrounded by those dearest and nearest to him.

Jedi began to feel that he was dealing, not with a human being, but with a kind of psychopath. The boy had no sense of right and wrong, no human feelings and no compassion. By not contacting Jedi during the last two months, he had led him to believe that the whole thing was over. And then just as he was feeling most confident and happy he had struck another deadly blow. This blow was even more deadly than the previous one because Jedi was now fairly certain that this thing would go on indefinitely.

Jedi realized that if this blackmail continued he would be completely ruined. He was well off and had a good salary, but he was certainly not wealthy and his funds were not inexhaustible. He started having visions of having to sell or mortgage his house in order to satisfy Abdul's demands. He was damned if he would sell this beautiful house on this most beautiful spot in Freetown. He had built it with his own resources, out of his own hard labor. He would rather die. This thought stiffened his backbone. He would simply have to find some means of dealing with this evil monster.

As his spirits rose, Jedi rose from his chair, gritted his teeth, clenched his fists and started pacing the length of the balcony as if this would aid the process of finding the means of combating Abdul. It then occurred to Jedi that maybe Abdul did not so much want money as power over another individual, particularly an exalted individual like himself. The young man obviously enjoyed seeing a highly placed individual squirm. He was a big tree, and Abdul would like to see him fall. It was the usual attitude of the peasant who used whatever opportunity he had to compensate for his insignificance by watching a superior person brought low. But now he, Jedi, had made up his mind to frustrate Abdul's enjoyment. He was going to devise a strategy. He was sure he could do it.

As he made this resolution, Jedi stamped his right foot ferociously on the floor, and as, in his pacing, he had just come to one end of the balcony, he swirled around to face the other end, lifted his head, and froze to the spot. The terror he had felt the previous night when he took Abdul's first phone call was nothing compared to what he was feeling now. His knees wobbled and that liquid was surely trickling down his right leg again. His stomach churned and his mouth went completely dry. If he could have seen his own face, he would have realized that he looked like death. His mouth was half open as though he were about to ask a question and his eyes were just two slits, like the half open eyes on the faces of some mummies. His face would have made the perfect specimen for a study in terror.

What had Jedi seen? Nothing less than two policemen in uniform walking up from the intersection towards his house. The sight of two policemen would not normally have been anything to worry about. Policemen quite often walked about the streets and at times, in pairs. In fact, if they were going to investigate a particular affair they usually went in pairs. Even if one were aware of some wrongdoing, the sight of two policemen would not necessarily cause undue consternation, because it was quite likely that they were going elsewhere: maybe to the hideouts of currency counterfeiters, drug dealers, brewers of illicit gin, or receivers of stolen goods. But Jedi was none of those. So why did he freeze to the spot with terror? It was because the two policemen were walking on either side of Abdul. Yes! Abdul was coming to his house accompanied by two policemen. That could mean only one thing: Abdul had finally gone to the police and made a report and the two policemen were coming to arrest him and charge him with murder.

He had known this vicious and demonic young man would do something terrible in revenge for his having hung up on him last night, but it had not occurred to him that he would go this far. Jedi faced the real prospect that he would be tried, convicted of murder, sentenced to death and hanged. From now on life would be unimaginable terror and misery, and would probably culminate in a disgraceful death. He realized that these were probably the last moments that he would spend in this beautiful house that he had planned and built himself and given an appropriate name. It held so many pleasurable memories for him and contained his most prized possessions and precious documents. Was he about to leave it forever?

By this time Abdul and the two policemen had entered the compound through the gate and climbed the steps leading to the porch and front door. Jedi heard the door bell ring three times. It sounded worse than the ringing of the telephone the previous night, and struck him as a harbinger of death. He knew that Juldeh would soon let the three messengers of death into his lounge downstairs and that they would soon have their clutches on him. What could he do? He felt like pleading, *"Please, death, give me time to collect my thoughts, to put my house in order, to put a few things together: a toothbrush and toothpaste, some money, some documents, toilet roll, an overnight bag: anything!"* But Juldeh was already at his bedroom door, telling him that there were two policemen and another man downstairs asking for him. So it was really happening. He wasn't going to wake up and find it had been a bad dream. And to think that they had chosen to come on a Sunday of all days, when God-fearing people were at church praising their maker! And it had to be on this particular Sunday, when he had asked Juldeh to come to work! He was going to be arrested and carted off to prison in the presence of his houseboy! The news would soon be all over the town.

Juldeh was absolutely amazed by his boss's behavior. It was as though Jedi hadn't heard a word he said even though he was looking straight at him. His master's mouth was half open, his knees and hands seemed to be shaking, and there was a ghastly expression on his face. If Juldeh had known what the policemen had come for, he would have concluded there and then that his master was guilty. He had to repeat his statement three times before Jedi reacted.

"Okay, tell them I am coming," he said in a faint voice.

It then occurred to Jedi that it would be humiliating for Juldeh to hear what were bound to be sordid exchanges between himself, on the one hand, and Abdul and the policemen on the other. He knew what that thug was capable of; he would deliberately seek to humiliate him in front of his steward. So Jedi said, as Juldeh was going down the steps, "By the way, you can go home for the day now."

There was a look of surprise on Juldeh's face as he said, "But boss, I have not yet finished the cleaning up."

"Oh, it can wait until tomorrow. Go now."

Juldeh was intelligent enough to realize that something was about to transpire that his employer did not want him to witness. He recalled the vulgar language he had heard over the telephone during the party and concluded that that event was related to whatever was about to happen now. Being inquisitive by nature, Juldeh would have given his right hand to be present at the ensuing confrontation, so that he would be able to relate it, with various embellishments, to his friends and relatives later. But his boss had given an order and he thought it best to comply.

Jedi waited till he was sure that Juldeh was safely off the scene before he went downstairs to meet his visitors. He had tried as much as possible to regain some composure so as not to give an impression of guilt. On entering the lounge into which Juldeh had ushered them, he said good morning out of mere politeness and sat down. He noticed that the policemen were already comfortably seated, one of them on his best chair, with one leg crossed over the other as if he were the master of the house. Abdul was also seated in a plush soft recliner and was comfortably enjoying a cigarette. Fancy that dog, that rat from the sewers of King Jimmy, sitting on one of his expensive chairs and smoking a cigarette in his lounge without so much as asking his permission! And the policemen had not even bothered to greet him as he entered the lounge. They obviously belonged almost to the lowest ranks and under normal circumstances would have risen when he entered and addressed him as "sir." Now from the expression on their faces it was obvious that they considered *him* to be the lowest of the low, little better than some gutter rat. The humiliation had already started and Jedi was already stung by it. But he did not hold the bargaining chips and he would have to be patient.

"Mr. Thomas," said one of the policemen, "I am Police Constable Demoh. This is Police Constable Bayoh. Do you know this young man?"

Jedi had been careful to avoid Abdul's eyes since he came into the lounge. He now threw a look at him that clearly said, "You dirty scum! So you have done it at last!"

He wondered whether he should deny knowing him, decided that there would be no point in doing that, so he said vaguely,

"I have seen him before."

"Well, Mr. Thomas, this young man, Abdul Sanusi, has reported that you have done something very bad! Something horrible, nasty, unmentionable! Something so bad that the whole country would rise up against you if they knew and demand that you pay the severest penalty the law prescribes! He can produce a lot of evidence, and he even suggests that he himself might have become a victim of your terrible crimes. He has not yet told us exactly what it is because he is a good man who would prefer to avoid scandal. And, in a sense, it is probably not wise for us to know what it is because then we would have no choice but to take you down to the station, charge you, and bring you to trial."

Jedi was both relieved and astonished. So Abdul had not told them about Emma's death, but he was holding out the possibility that he would if Jedi did not do as they wanted. What did they want? Money, of course. He should have guessed. Abdul did not want his death as yet. He would keep that threat dangling over his head like the sword of Damocles, but only use it when he felt there was nothing more to be gained from him.

"So this man has not accused me of anything specific?" Jedi asked. "You must know that it is illegal for you to come to my house and say someone has accused me of a crime without saying what the crime is. Are you going to charge me with not having done anything specific? This is ridiculous. What do you want?"

"Mr. Thomas," said Abdul coolly, "you know, and you know that I know, that you are a wicked, filthy, nasty man who does not deserve the position you hold in this town. You know of the unpardonable things you have done. You know! And I know! And you know that I know! You know that at one time you actually tried to pay me to remain quiet. You know that if I open my mouth your whole life will be destroyed because you have done things that the law condemns and will punish most severely. So don't try to bluff. Just listen to what we have come to offer."

"And what is that?"

"Abdul here," Constable Bayoh said, "is prepared to shut his mouth and forget the whole thing, if you give him one million leones. Although he has good evidence and good cause, he knows it is not always wise to fight a big man. You might be in a position to do something good for him one day. But one million leones is the least he will accept."

Jedi sprang from his chair, shouting, "One million leones! Do you people think I am a millionaire? Where do you expect me to get all that money?"

"Mr. Thomas," said Constable Demoh, "Sit down. Don't you realize that you have as good as admitted that you committed a terrible crime?" He turned to Abdul with a proper air of moral outrage.

"Mr Sanusi, I don't think we should play around with this man anymore. Let us do the proper thing and take him to the Central Police Station where you will state the charges against him and we will formally charge him."

"I for one don't want to stay in this house one moment longer," Constable Bayoh agreed. "It stinks. It is clear that filthy things have been done here and I don't want to be polluted. Let us go to the station."

At this, Jedi almost fell on his knees, pleading. "Wait, wait, wait!"

The last thing he wanted was to go to the police station and have charges of any kind made against him, charges that were likely to include murder. The one million leones was probably going to be shared among the three of them. That was what the police were like. Unspeakably corrupt! But for now he would just have to comply. It was his very life that was on the line.

"Okay," he said. "Will you take a cheque?"

"You know we are officers of the law, so you will not dare to do anything funny with the cheque; I mean you will not give us a cheque that will bounce or anything like that," said Constable Demoh.

"Of course not," Jedi replied. "I am a man of honor. And I hope you will be men of honor and ensure that this thing stops here. I have no more money. This young man has absolutely fleeced me."

"We are police officers and we give you our word," said Constable Bayoh. "This young man wanted to press charges but we advised him that he should come to some kind of accommodation with you. Now that he has done that, we are here to witness it and to sanction it and see that he stands by it. You can consider the matter closed."

As Jedi was about to go upstairs to write the cheque, Constable Bayoh called out, "Bring me some water before you go up."

Jedi was so taken aback that he almost hit his toe against one of the steps. Was this nonentity of a policeman ordering him about in his own house? Had he never heard of the word "please"? However, recalling that they had behaved throughout as though they had the upper hand, as indeed they had, he carried out the order without protest.

CHAPTER 6

Seventy year-old Mama Sawyerr was one of Jedi's neighbors. She lived in a modest but attractive one-storey house on pillars that had been built for her by her devoted son who had been away in the United States for the past fifteen years making his fortune and trying to achieve the American dream. She lived with two of her grandchildren who were in their late teens and were attending secondary school. Her grandchildren did most of the shopping and whatever chores needed to be done about the house, while Mama Sawyerr did most of the cooking and tried to bring up the children in the way they should go. She had a lot of leisure time on her hands, and most of that time she spent sitting in her most comfortable chair on the verandah or in the lounge, discreetly hidden behind one of her voluminous curtains. From both vantage points she was able to survey most of what was happening in the neighborhood. She had not been invited to Jedi's party, and this was still rankling with her on that Sunday morning. At seventy, she did not think she would have been able to take part in the dancing, but she would have sat around and enjoyed the fun, the food and the drinks. That Jedidiah Thomas probably thought she was not good enough to be invited to mingle with all his high-up friends.

So on this Sunday morning Mama Sawyerr was in an angry mood as she sat on the verandah. She was so angry that she decided not to go to church as she would normally have done on a Sunday morning. Mama Sawyerr was extremely religious, and she firmly believed that before going up to the altar to partake in the celebration of the Lord's Supper she should be in love and charity with all men. But she could not forgive Jedi for not inviting her to his party, so she did not go to church that Sunday. She decided to sit there and call out loudly to Jedi as he drove by on his way to church to remind him of her existence and make him feel guilty for not inviting her. She sat there for hours, but Jedi's car did not emerge from his garage. That meant he was not going to church either. So after a night of revelry, gluttony and debauchery he had not thought it fit to go and worship his maker and pray for forgiveness for his excesses! What was the world coming to?

As such self-righteous thoughts were going through Mama Sawyerr's mind, she turned and saw a wonder of wonders coming up the road. There were two policemen and another young man coming up their street. Mama Sawyerr had never been involved with the law before, but she knew that whenever you saw two policemen going somewhere together, you could be sure that they were going to investigate a crime or make an arrest. But everyone who lived on their street was highly respectable, so what could those policemen be coming to investigate? Mama Sawyerr was even more astonished when she saw the policemen and the other man go into Jedidiah Thomas's compound. What could the man have done? Of course, some sort of evil had resulted from all that elbow bending last night. And Jedidiah Thomas had not even bothered to go to church to pray this morning. Something bad was bound to come out of affronting the Lord in this way. She was going to get to the bottom of it, even if it meant bribing the steward. To start her investigation, she went into her bedroom and hung her head out of the window that was most adjacent to Jedi's wall to see whether she could hear anything of the proceedings inside.

Mama Sawyerr's suspicions were confirmed when, a few minutes after the policemen went into Jedi's compound, she saw Juldeh, leaving, with his usual suspicious-looking bag tucked under his right arm. That meant he was going home for good that day. This was strange, since he had arrived only a short while earlier. It must mean that Jedi was getting him out of the way and that something was happening in that house which Jedi did not want his steward to hear. As a man sows, she said to herself, so shall he reap. Jedi had certainly sowed a lot of wild things last night; now he was going to pay. Mama Sawyerr decided that she would try to get as much information out of Juldeh as she could, so she hurried back on to the verandah and called out to the young man.

"Howdo-oh, Juldeh! I have never seen you here on Sundays before."

"Morning ma! I don't usually work on Sundays, but boss asked me to come early today so I could do the cleaning after his party."

"So your master had a party last night! I heard the noise and the enjoyment. You people must really have enjoyed yourself. Did your master get engaged or something?"

"No ma; it was his birthday. He was fifty years old," Juldeh replied, thinking,

"This woman is a big busybody. She wants to know everything that is going on in everybody's house. I must be careful what I say."

"So," Mama Sawyer went on, "have you finished the cleaning already? You must work very fast."

"Yes, ma; I work very fast," Juldeh said, again thinking, *The old witch wants to know why my boss asked me to leave early. I won't tell her anything.*

"By the way," Mama Sawyerr persisted, "I saw two policemen going into your compound just now. I hope nothing was stolen during the party and all your boss's possessions are intact."

Stupid woman, thought Juldeh. *She is desperate to find out what the policemen are doing in my boss's house, but I shall show her that I am not a fool.* Aloud he said,

"Oh, nothing happened, ma. Everything is okay. I think some things were stolen from Mr. Thomas's office in town on Friday night or yesterday morning. The police wanted to get a statement from him as to what was missing, and he asked them to come to his house today because that was the time he would be at home."

A likely story! thought Mama Sawyer. *He is trying to cover up for his master. Something must definitely be wrong."* Aloud she said,

"Juldeh, I kept foofoo and some delicious okra soup for you yesterday. Come in and get it."

Now she is trying to bribe me, thought Juldeh. *I will eat her foofoo and okra, but she will get nothing out of me.*

"Keep it for me till tomorrow, ma. I am not going straight home. I shall collect it first thing in the morning, and enjoy it for my lunch. Goodbye, ma."

Mama Sawyerr had to give up.

"Goodbye-oh, Juldeh," she said.

When he had gone, she hurried back into the bedroom and glued her ears to the window once more, but she could hear nothing distinctly. Voices were raised and then lowered, and at one point she thought Jedi's voice was definitely pleading, while the policeman's sounded confident, assertive and demanding. Something fishy was definitely going on in that house. She would have given anything to know what it was all about.

After a while the young man and the policemen emerged once more. They seemed to be rejoicing over something. What were they gloating over? They could certainly not have been taking any statements. That would surely be no cause for such elation. Mama Sawyerr hid herself in a corner of her verandah where they could not see her but she would be able to overhear everything they were saying.

"Did you see his face," said one of the policemen as he laughed out boisterously. "I thought he was going to faint."

"I don't know about fainting," said the other, "but he was terrified out of his wits. Did you see piss dripping down his leg?"

"Yeah, man, he was pissing in his trousers. Did you watch him when we mentioned the money?"

"I thought he was going to hit the ceiling," replied his companion, and all of them roared with laughter.

"That is why one should always behave well. These big men! They think they can do anything they like and get away with it. They do all kinds of wicked and nasty things and believe no one will call them to account. Tomorrow he will dress up in his suit and tie and go to his office and start barking orders and expecting people like us to call him "sir", as though nothing has happened.

"Do you know," Abdul interjected, "one of the greatest pleasures I have in life is to watch a big man squirming. I am sure that in your job you have moments like that. Doesn't it give you a feeling of power when you see one of them holding your feet and begging for mercy, knowing that his fate is in your hands? Not even the pleasure I get from a woman beats that."

Mama Sawyerr was pleasantly shocked. She had guessed that something fishy was cooking in that house, but she hardly suspected it would be as serious as this. From what she had overheard from the policemen and their accomplice, Mr. Thomas was in big trouble. She did not know exactly what it was as yet, but she would surely find out; she had her methods. It would make extremely good gossip at next Friday's meeting of the Mothers' Union.

Meanwhile, the butt of their jokes and the centerpiece of their thoughts was writhing on his bed in misery and terror. After Abdul and the policemen left, Jedi went straight to his bedroom, poured himself a liberal helping of whisky and collapsed on his bed, moaning. It was quite obvious to him that Abdul's intention was not just to extort money from him, but to intimidate and terrorize him, maybe even to reduce him to abject submission. The only bright spot in the whole messy affair, if it could be called a bright spot, was the fact that Abdul had not told the policemen about the murder. And he would not tell them about the murder, not only because that would mean giving up his trump card, but also because the moment the policemen heard about a murder they were bound to come and arrest the suspect. Abdul obviously did not want him arrested as yet. He was not yet ready to surrender the goose that laid the golden egg. He wanted to force more money out of him and realize the power he had over him.

There could have been no better way of terrorizing him than to bring two policemen to his house on a Sunday morning. But then, the policemen had to be told that Jedi had committed an offence serious enough to warrant a visit to his house. What had Abdul told them? Of course! It now became quite clear. Abdul had told the policemen that he, Jedi, had committed or tried to commit, an act of gross indecency with him. The more he recalled what the policemen said, the more certain he was that that was what Abdul had told them. Hadn't they gone on and on about nasty and filthy acts? And it would make much more sense that they would allow him to bribe his way out of such an allegation than out of an allegation of murder. The policemen had said that Abdul had not specified the nature of the offence. That must have been a lie. Few policemen would act, even if it were to blackmail the suspect, if they had not been given some idea of the nature of the offence. Abdul must have fabricated the charge of gross indecency, but must also have let them know that his intention was not to arrest but to frighten Jedi into giving them money.

But why would Abdul insist that the nature of the crime should not be specified when they confronted Jedi? He knew, of course, that the moment "gross indecency" was mentioned Jedi would refute it and probably refuse to pay up. So he had to make Jedi believe that he was thinking of murder, while the policemen thought that he was talking about something else. It was a brilliant idea to let the crime remain unspecified. But then why would the policemen agree not to mention the exact nature of the crime to Jedi? It would reinforce the notion of their being merely intermediaries trying to get Jedi and Abdul to come to an accommodation. They assumed that Jedi would think policemen had an obligation to investigate a specific allegation, but that without one they were well within their rights merely to try to bring about an accommodation. Jedi could not therefore accuse them of complicity in extortion.

Jedi had to admit that he had seriously underestimated Abdul. He was a genius of sorts and had, in fact, played with all of them. The policemen almost certainly did not know that they were getting involved in a murder case, but the discussion had proceeded in such a way, that if murder turned up later, Abdul could say that he had been talking about murder all along but the policemen had misunderstood him. To think that this gutter rat had succeeded in twisting them around his little finger! No wonder old people had a saying that it is the mangy dog that kills the leopard. Was he, a veritable leopard, going to allow a mangy dog like Abdul to plague him, rob him of his hard-earned assets and finally kill him? Would it not be wise, after all, to seek legal advice, some kind of advice anyway? After all, he was a big man with important connections. Surely, he should be able to mobilize more resources than that miserable worm and go on the offensive.

Later that afternoon the doorbell rang again. Jedi sprang out of bed as if he had been suddenly bitten on the buttocks. The sound of a bell or of anything ringing now had that effect on him. He relaxed somewhat when he realized that it was the doorbell and not the telephone, and proceeded to go downstairs, thinking it might be a friend coming to find out why he was not in church that morning. He would not be surprised if it was those busybodies, Ethan Spencer and Elkanah Pratt. To say that they were interested in last night's telephone calls would be an understatement. They had probably come to see whether they could ferret anything out of him; but he was prepared for them.

He opened the door. Instead of Ethan and Elkanah, Abdul stood before him, grinning. The cheek of the swine, after extorting one million leones from him! What did he want now?

"How dare you come here again after what you did to me this morning?" Jedi snapped, glaring at him.

Abdul sighed like a schoolmaster confronting an unteachable pupil. "Why can't you learn, Mr. Thomas? When will you realize that I am now your master and you must never talk to me like that? Are we going to raise our voices? If that is what you want I can raise my voice and alert the whole neighborhood. I am sure they will be pleased to know about your shameful behavior."

Abdul then brushed past Jedi and went into the lounge uninvited. He sought out the most comfortable chair, sat down, crossed his legs, lit a cigarette, and nonchalantly started to puff out smoke rings. Outraged by this further evidence of Abdul's insolence, Jedi again raised his voice.

"I don't allow smoking in here. You should at least have asked my permission."

"Ask your permission?" Abdul's incredulous scream suggested that Jedi had just said something completely stupid.

"Where have you ever heard of the master asking the slave's permission? Anyone who has power of life and death over someone almost owns that person. If I own you, then it follows that I own whatever is yours. In this house, I will behave as I like and from now on, you take orders from me, Mr. Thomas. Get that into your head once and for all."

"*What* do you want from me?" Jedi fumed. "You are a thief and a liar. When I gave you six hundred thousand leones you told me that was the end of the matter and I could get on with my life in peace. Then you came here yesterday with two policemen demanding one million leones. What kind of devil are you?"

"Let us go over what we have both done, Mr. Thomas, and consider which of us is more wicked," Abdul replied coolly. "They say that only God and fools don't change. Well, I am certainly not God, and I am not a fool. Six hundred thousand leones was too small to pay for two lives; don't you think so Mr. Thomas? Also, you keep forcing me to remind you that I am your master."

Abdul paused for a minute, elegantly blew out more smoke rings, and admired them, before going on.

"You hung up on me yesterday, so I had to come to you today with those two policemen to show you that I mean business. *You* forced me to bring you to the attention of those policemen. They are now convinced that you are guilty of nasty crimes. If you refuse to do as I say, I shall go back to them and they will not hesitate to arrest and charge you. Once that happens, the whole thing will be in the open and out of my hands. There will be no going back."

Abdul's mention of "nasty crimes" reminded Jedi that while the policemen had not specified his offence, they seemed to be under the impression that he had committed some unspeakable acts. So he said to Abdul,

"You seem to have suggested to them that I was involved in some liaison with you. My God! Have you no shame? And how dare you try to make people believe that a man like me would be involved in such filth, and with riff-raff like you? Perhaps you are familiar with such things in the gutter you come from. *Not* me…

"Oh, Mr. Thomas," said Abdul with another weary sigh, "Why can't you learn? Why can't you accept that what you did to Emma was much worse than any liaison with me? Well, which do you prefer, to be accused of corrupting a teenager and of murder, or to be accused of indecent behavior? Take your pick."

It was Jedi's turn to heave a weary sigh, but this reflected his true state of mind. "So what do you want from me now?"

"Oh, nothing for the moment. One million leones will go a long way. I have only come to make sure you got the message of this morning: that the police now know about you and that if you refuse to do as I say I have the will and the means to get them to arrest you. And don't think I am making idle threats. I can do it. Bring me a beer."

Jedi boiled within at the insult, the arrogance and the cheek, but nevertheless went to bring Abdul a bottle of Heineken beer. While Abdul continued to smoke his cigarette, blowing out smoke rings, and enjoying his beer as though he were in his own home, Jedi silently regarded him with a mixture of disdain and horror, saying not a word.

Abdul eventually departed, leaving Jedi in no doubt that the financial demands were just starting. This thing was likely to go on and on. And now, there were two others involved. He just had to find some way of getting rid of this threat to his career, his resources, his happiness, and his life. After considering his options for about a week, Jedi decided that going away for a while would give him breathing space. He would also have time to think and could perhaps seek the advice of non-Sierra Leoneans who were less likely to give away his secret. Since he had accumulated several months of leave, he decided to take it and go to England for a while.

His application for three months leave was granted without delay as it was long overdue. Senior civil servants did not always take their leave in case the person acting in their position snooped out secrets that could have serious consequences if exposed. Quite a few senior civil servants had been destroyed in this way, and one way in which the President or an honorable minister got rid of a top civil servant was to order him to go on leave. Though much more straightforward than most of his colleagues, even Jedi had his bureaucratic secrets. Nevertheless, he felt that they were insignificant compared with the one in the possession of his arch-enemy. Their revelation would be a small price to pay for the peace of mind he would enjoy for a while.

He had a roundtrip ticket to the United Kingdom issued about nine months previously to allow himself and some other officials to attend a conference which had been called off at the last moment. Jedi and the others had been most annoyed, not because of the loss of intellectual stimulation that the conference would have provided, but because it meant losing a two-week per diem allowance which would have been paid in pounds sterling. However, as frequently happened where the government was concerned, whoever issued the tickets had forgotten to recall them, so not all was lost.

Jedi was glad that it was already spring in the United Kingdom, for he knew all about British winters. He had never forgotten one extremely cold evening when he was trying to study for an examination the next morning. His electric heater suddenly went out which meant he had to put more coins in the meter. To his dismay he discovered that he had none of the necessary coins. However, study he must, so he added to his vest and double-knit pullover, not only his thickest woolen suit but also his heavy winter coat. That way he had been able to keep warm enough to study late into the night. That was the kind of resourcefulness and dedication that had earned him his present position. It was the kind of thing that cockroach, Abdul, would never understand.

Jedi had arranged to stay with Edward a cousin who lived in Hammersmith, London, with his wife, Ekundayo. The moment he put down his suitcase Jedi breathed such a tremendous sigh that Edward had to ask if all was well. Of course, Jedi did not reveal that the sigh was one of relief due to the prospect of three months respite from Abdul's depredations. Instead he answered,

"Government work has been killing me, Eddie. For the next three months I intend to rest and enjoy myself without a care in the world. Let them do whatever they like in that office. I don't care. I can sleep when I want to, wake up when I want to, eat when I want to and go out when I want to. Three months of perfect freedom!"

So in the mornings after Edward and Ekundayo had gone to work, Jedi would continue resting in bed until about ten o'clock. Then he would make himself a heavy breakfast and watch television. Sometimes, he went to an afternoon movie or to visit one of the tourist attractions he remembered from his student days, mingled with other holiday-makers and felt on top of the world. He put on quite a bit of weight, and there was a renewed jauntiness to his walk. Not only had Abdul and the threat he posed receded into the distance, office concerns had also been removed from his shoulders. Besides, in London he did not have to put up with all those inconveniences contingent on living in Freetown: power cuts, telephones that mysteriously stopped working and could not be repaired until the technicians had received hefty bribes, gas and water shortages, and traffic hold-ups caused by some section of the road being "repaired" or some slow-moving funeral procession only yards ahead. Here everything was organized and orderly. If he went into a store to look for a pair of trousers or just to browse around he was promptly greeted by a smiling shop assistant with, "Good morning, sir! How may I help you, sir?" Here the customer was always right, and the politeness of the shop assistants forced one to buy something even though one might not have intended to on entering the store. Shopping in England was light-years away from the situation back home where some semi-literate shop assistant in an Indian or Lebanese-owned store hardly condescended to reply to your inquiries about the cost of an item you genuinely wanted to purchase and, when you finally did, behaved as though he was doing you a huge favor.

One afternoon, after his usual lazy morning, Jedi decided to go to a movie, just to pass the time. This was the essence of a vacation: to be able to go to a movie in the afternoon. The showing started at 2 pm, so Jedi entered the movie theatre at 1:45. He bought himself a coke and some popcorn, and settled comfortably into a well upholstered seat. The theatre was an enormous Victorian structure that could comfortably seat one thousand people, and since it was almost empty at that time of day, he almost felt as if the movie was being shown for his benefit alone. The ambience was simply wonderful. The movie itself was unremarkable, but it was a story about a blackmail with which Jedi could relate and he felt very satisfied as he walked home afterwards. In the end, both blackmailers had got what was coming to them and had been removed from the face of the earth. *It is a pity Abdul does not live in a place like London,* Jedi thought. *Here he would have been history by now.* However, he soon swept Abdul from his thoughts, reminding himself that he had come to London to forget about him. He should not let Abdul trouble his mind even slightly on a day when he had had an unusually satisfying experience in an English cinema theatre.

CHAPTER 7

Jedi returned home mentally revitalized and physically invigorated. He had brought presents for several relations and friends and various items he needed for himself. Another person would undoubtedly have had to pay thousands of leones or heavy bribes to some of the customs officials in order to have their duty reduced, but not Jedidiah Thomas, Permanent Secretary. It was not that officials like him were exempt from paying customs duty; far from it. It was simply that if one was sufficiently important or had enough contacts one got away with not paying. In Jedi's case the customs officials were sycophantic in their effusive welcome and their congratulations to him for having returned home safely after a splendid vacation.

"You are very heartily welcome back, sir," one of them gushed. "I hope your vacation was highly enjoyable, sir."

"I hope you had a comfortable flight back, sir," another chimed in.

Radiating bonhomie and good fellowship, Jedi returned their compliments and thanked them. He enquired after their health and hoped that life was being good to them.

"Mr. Sellu," shouted the supervising officer, "please chalk Mr. Thomas's bags."

"Yes, sir!"

And it was done. Mr. Sellu chalk-marked each of Jedi's bags with an initial that looked like 'S' to indicate that they had been thoroughly inspected and contained no prohibited or dutiable goods, or that whatever dutiable goods they contained had been fully paid for. Jedi grunted with satisfaction. Yes! This was the way things should be done. A man in his position deserved to be treated with deference and respect, not like the 'hoi polloi'. You had to know how to work the system in order to benefit from it. Jedi knew that these officials were not performing acts of kindness or respect. A man in Jedi's position had either helped them in the past or would be able to help them in the future. Indeed, Jedi had used his position, contacts, and authority to get some of them appointed or promoted over the heads of much better qualified candidates, and he had done so because he knew that they too, in their turn, would help him when he needed their assistance. He had brought presents for them, too—a half bottle of brandy here, a pocket calculator there—to induce them to pretend that he did not owe the government and people of Sierra Leone anything for his dutiable items. That was the way things were done. The officials accepted his gifts with smiles. Mr. Thomas was a man who knew how to do business.

"Oh, Mr. Thomas," exclaimed his secretary, Mrs. Cole, when he reported for work a week later, "you look so young and fresh!"

Saying that one looked fresh was another way of pointing out that one had put on a few pounds. Jedi's waistline had certainly expanded. Other cultures might regard that as an unhealthy sign, but in Sierra Leone it was a sign of health, wealth, and importance. People never told the individual in question that he had put on weight; they said he looked fresh.

"Thank you Mrs. Cole," Jedi answered, beaming. "I do feel great. My relations and friends in the U.K. fed me well and the rest has done me a world of good."

"The very change of air and the good breezes in a country like that would be enough to make anyone look young and rosy," remarked another female member of his staff. "Were it not for my family, I would just pack my bags and go and live there permanently; then I would not have to put up with all the inconveniences and harassment in this God-forsaken country."

"Those are true words that you have spoken," a male office worker observed. "The moment I have saved enough money, I will buy a one-way ticket to England and go and live with my brother's wife's cousin in Liverpool."

The mention of inconveniences and harassment made Jedi wince, though imperceptibly. The woman had reminded him of Abdul and the terror from which he had fled to England. During his blissful three-month absence from Freetown, Abdul had become little more than a distant and little-remembered nightmare. Now, he re-entered his mind, but Jedi was feeling so reinvigorated that he was sure he could cope with any threat or challenge that Abdul could now pose. That was the beauty of going to a place like England: one recharged one's batteries. He was sure he could walk four or five miles without becoming tired; that he could lift and carry a bag of rice effortlessly and, if need be, pulverize Abdul. Yes! That was the way to deal with a chap like Abdul: thrash him within an inch of his life; then he would know who was master.

At home, Jedi spent the two weeks or so after his return receiving and returning calls welcoming him back and congratulating him on his safe return and his generally healthy and imposing appearance. He was perfectly in his element and thoroughly enjoyed the situation. He smiled and guffawed good-naturedly as he responded to questions and discussed the most interesting aspects of his vacation.

"You rascal," he said to Ethan Spencer when that friend telephoned him. "You have such a one-track mind. Do you think that all one does in England is to chase women?"

"Of course," replied Ethan. "We go to UK for rejuvenation and women do that best, especially the juvies. A chap like you ought to know that."

Jedi winced again, for Ethan's remark brought bad memories. What on earth did he mean by that?

"Don't you know what 'rejuvenation' means? Ethan went on, quite unaware of the discomfort he was causing his friend. "It means allowing oneself to be inspired and revitalized by sweet young things."

Jedi pretended to enjoy the joke, but he was thinking, *Trust the rogue to give the word his own salacious meaning.*

Throughout those two weeks he enjoyed taking calls and recounting his experiences. Then came the day when the phone rang and the caller was someone he had hoped never to hear from again.

"Welcome back juvie murderer!"

For a moment, Jedi froze; then his confidence returned and he resolved to deal with Abdul ruthlessly, once and for all.

"Look here, you damn thief!" he yelled into the receiver, "I have had enough of you. Get off my phone right now or I will make you curse your mother, and the very day you were born. I will *smash* you to smithereens."

Slightly taken aback by the violence of Jedi's response, Abdul did not reply immediately.

"Did you hear what I said, you thief?" Jedi demanded.

"Yes I did, Mr. Murderer. But it seems as if you have forgotten yourself. I think I will have to remind you. I will be visiting you very soon to demand my own gift from the U K."

"If you value your life, don't come near me," Jedi warned, before realizing that Abdul had hung up.

Abdul's silence for the two weeks since his return had fooled Jedi into thinking that the threat had disappeared. He now realized the truth of what he had heard so many times: that blackmail will continue until the blackmailer is stopped. Well, he would stop Abdul, even if he had to use physical force. He would thrash him himself or hire thugs to do it. He would make Abdul realize that if he continued his predatory activities he would become badly disfigured and of no further use to women. That was the only way to treat him. A plan was already beginning to form in his mind.

Bolstered by this new confidence, Jedi went to church the next morning and praised his maker with great enthusiasm. Some of his fellow parishioners noticed the new bounce in his walk, the new glint in his eye, his radiant expression, and put them down to his three-month long vacation in the UK. After the service, he went with other sidesmen to the home of one of their group for lunch and beer before returning to Juba Hill. He took a short nap and then came out on to his upstairs balcony to laze the time away on his hammock and enjoy the magnificent view. What looked like a cruise ship was turning into the estuary from the ocean, and he admired the grace and majesty of the vessel as it glided over the water. The atmosphere was serenely peaceful that Sunday afternoon, and Jedi felt he was part of that serenity and peace. He turned his gaze away from the sea for a moment to take in the lofty mountains in the distance. Instead, his eyes landed on the unwelcome sight of two uniformed policemen walking up the road towards his house. They recognized him, smiled, and waved. *God in heaven!* Jedi thought. *It is those criminals! What are they coming for?* They had assured him that they would never bother him again. Indeed, they had promised to guarantee that Abdul did not bother him again. Not only had they failed to do that, they were obviously here to torment him themselves. Or were they coming to arrest him? Had Abdul sent them? In their conversation the night before Abdul had made his usual threats. Was the cat finally going to devour the mouse having toyed with him to his satisfaction? As he panicked, it occurred to Jedi to go into his bedroom and pretend that he was not at home; but he soon dismissed that idea. The policemen had seen him. They had even smiled and waved to him. He would just have to go downstairs and let them in.

They greeted him politely and he invited them to sit down. Constable Demoh stretched out his legs and placed his dirty shoes on the center table, while Constable Bayoh swung his right leg over the arm of Jedi's best chair. They then proceeded to chat as companionably as if they were his friends, enquiring about the details of his trip abroad. However, after a few minutes of this, Constable Demoh ordered Jedi to bring him a beer.

Again, Jedi was taken aback by the sudden change of tone from this man who, just a moment before, had been talking to him like a genial friend.

"And *I* will take a brandy and ginger ale," added Constable Bayoh in the same peremptory tone.

In normal circumstances, low level policemen like these would not have dared to come to his house uninvited, let alone expect to be offered a drink. Now here they were, behaving as though he was their servant. It was that dog Abdul who had reduced him to such indignities. But he would show him.

Jedi seethed inwardly but had no alternative but to carry out their wishes. Neither of the two policemen had the good manners even to mutter a "thank you!" Instead, they both took cigarettes from their pockets. Constable Demoh issued another order.

"Bring me a match."

This meant one more trip to the kitchen where Juldeh kept matches to light the kerosene stove whenever there was a power outage. However, Jedi went to fetch the matches without a word and offered the box to Constable Demoh. Instead of taking it, Constable Demoh put the cigarette to his lips and pushed it toward Jedi.

So, thought Jedi, *they now expect me to light their cigarettes for them.*

Again he complied and did the same for Constable Bayoh.

For a few minutes the two men said nothing more; just sat there in his comfortable chairs and smoked contentedly, polluting the normally fragrant air.

"*Oh God,*" thought Jedi, "*must I endure this?*

Up to this point he had been quietly waiting for the policemen to get to the point of the visit. At last Constable Demoh deigned to speak.

"Well Mr. Thomas," he began, "you know that young man you have the problem with?"

Jedi was alarmed that he said "have" rather than "had," thus suggesting that the problem was not over.

"Well, he has not stopped pestering us during these three months you have been away. He said you must have run away, and blamed us for letting you escape. He said that if we had not persuaded him to come to an accommodation with you, he would certainly have got you arrested and charged so you could pay for committing such a crime."

"That is the truth," said Constable Bayoh. "We tried to reason with him. We even said that your going away to a foreign country might be the best solution to the problem, so we could all forget the whole thing and get on with our lives and allow you to get on with yours. But he said he had been reading about crimes and their investigation and he had realized that if it was discovered that you were involved in such a serious crime and he knew about it and did not report it to the police and get you arrested, he might be charged with participating in a cover up. He felt this was exactly what he had done and it was tormenting him badly. He said he could not sleep at night, worrying about it. He said he had never before been in trouble with the police. He had always tried to live a straightforward and honest life and had always done what his mother and grandmother had taught him to do. He said he felt he had no alternative but to redeem himself and make a clean breast of everything to the police."

"When we pointed out to him the difficulty of proceeding against you while you were in the UK," said Constable Demoh, "he said that from what he understood there would be no problem in having you arrested there and sent back to Sierra Leone.. He said he even preferred that, because you would then be exposed and disgraced not only before your friends and relations in Sierra Leone, but also before your friends over there"

Sweat had broken out all over Jedi's forehead at the mention of arrest, extradition, exposure and disgrace. Constable Bayoh noticed that he was almost shaking and spoke with a slight smile of satisfaction when he took over the narrative.

"We even reminded him that we had given our word that we would not bother you again after you gave us that substantial sum the last time: we had been the guarantors that that would be the end of the matter; and that we were men of honor."

"Honor is very important to us as policemen," Constable Demoh interjected. "What respect will the public have for policemen if they feel that we cannot be trusted? I am jealous of my honor and my truthfulness and I will defend them with my life."

"You have said the truth, my brother," said Constable Bayoh. "So we tried to reason with him, but he was adamant. He even tried to teach us our work, saying that our duty as policemen demanded that when we heard about a serious crime we should investigate it and see that justice was done. It was not our business to reconcile the parties concerned. He said his conscience had been tormenting him and even hinted that he was considering reporting the matter to our superintendent. Can you imagine that, sir? That small boy implying that we had failed in our duty, when all we were trying to do was to help him, and all because of you, sir!"

"Mr. Thomas," Constable Demoh said in his turn, "There have been several nights when I could not sleep because I was afraid that Abdul would betray us to our superiors. And then what would become of us? We both have wives and children. If we are dismissed from the force, how will they eat? Who will pay the school fees? If I lose my job, where will I get money? You see the risk we have taken for you?"

"And, as you know, he is a devilish kind of boy," said Constable Bayoh. "At times he hangs around the station just to remind us that he is there. Believe me, Mr. Thomas, there are times when I almost piss in my trousers when I see him. On several occasions we have had to take money out of our own pockets and pay him, just to keep him quiet. Last month almost the whole of my salary went to him. My wife and children almost starved."

Constable Bayoh seemed close to tears and his partner took over in a similarly mournful tone.

"Believe me, Mr. Thomas, this world is wicked! You should never do good for people; they will turn against you. Rather, do good for a dog; at least it will show gratitude."

"And people are at their most wicked when they know they have information that could destroy you," Constable Bayoh added for good measure.

Jedi could not help admiring the effrontery and acting skills of the two men. He could see through their ploy: pretend that they were suffering and had lost a lot of money and peace of mind all because they had tried to do their best for him out of the goodness of their hearts. All of it leading up to extorting more money from him. The only thing he was not sure about was whether they had come on their own initiative or at Abdul's instigation. Whatever money they extorted from him they would probably share with Abdul. Instead of paying one person, he now had to pay three. At this rate he would soon be bankrupt. On the other hand, was it remotely possible that some of what they said could be true? Had Abdul really threatened to tell their superintendent? Might the superintendent himself be brought into the conspiracy? If so, he was done for.

But he still made no comment and let the two constables ramble on. He would not say anything that could incriminate him.

"Abdul went to see us yesterday and asked us what we intended to do," Constable Demoh went on. "Were we going to arrest you now that you had come back from England? We had to plead with him. Can you imagine that, sir? Big men like us. Believe me, that boy knows how to use his power. We are all at his mercy now. And all because we tried to help! We had to go down on our knees and beg him to give us some time. I tell you, that boy enjoys torturing people. He will torture all of us, and my wife and children are already starving."

"My own wife has threatened to leave me," Constable Bayoh chimed in. "We will have to give him something really substantial this time to persuade him not to go to the superintendent."

Jedi knew it was time to speak.

"About how much?"

"Two million leones," Constable Demoh replied."

"Two million leones!" Jedi protested as vehemently as he had done on the previous occasion. "Where do you people expect me to get it?"

"Mr. Thomas," said Constable Bayoh in as stern a tone as he could summon, "do you know how much we have spent trying to pacify that boy while you were enjoying yourself in England? In addition to the two million leones for Abdul, you will have to pay us the five hundred thousand we spent out of our own pockets to keep him quiet. The total sum is two million five hundred thousand."

"You people must be out of your minds," Jedi told him bitterly. "Do you know how much money I spent on my ticket and paying for my expenses in England? I am flat broke at the moment."

As soon as he mentioned his trip to England, Jedi realized that he had made a mistake. It was Constable Demoh's turn to shout, and he did so loudly enough for Jedi's neighbors to hear.

"We are not interested in your expensive trip to England, Mr. Thomas. You have to take responsibility for your wicked and immoral actions here in Freetown. That is what we are concerned about, and we have to protect ourselves. Constable Bayoh, let us arrest this man, as we should have done long ago. Let us arrest him before Abdul goes and reports us to the superintendent and before we lose our jobs in disgrace. Mr. Jedidiah Thomas, we must ask you to come with us to the Central Police Station where you will find Abdul Sanusi ready and willing to substantiate the charges against you."

On seeing the two policemen rise to their feet, Jedi panicked. He was quite sure that that busybody Mama Sawyerr was already looking out of her window to see what was going on in his house, and that if he left the building with the policemen the news would soon be all over town that he had been arrested. Moreover, the words "police station" were the last thing Jedi wanted to hear, knowing that if he went down to the Central Police Station he was finished. He had no alternative but to demean himself before these two scoundrels, and beg for mercy.

"Please, please, don't be hasty," he said hurriedly and as humbly as he could. "I shall try to satisfy you even if it means withdrawing all my savings."

The two policemen exchanged glances as though questioning whether to make further concessions to this crab, whether they should risk their jobs and reputations for him; then Constable Bayoh said with an air of doing Jedi a huge favor.

"Okay, we will accept the two million five hundred thousand leones. Maybe we'll be able to pacify Abdul. But we are not promising anything; you know how devilish and determined he is." He added sanctimoniously, "Demoh and I always try to do all we can to help our fellow human beings. Whenever we see someone in deep trouble, we try to help him. If everyone were like us, the world would be a much better place.

Fifteen minutes later, Jedi handed him a cheque for two million five hundred thousand leones. It would probably be scraping the bottom of the barrel of his savings, but there was nothing else to do.

"By the way," Constable Bayoh said as they made their way outside, "my first cousin on my mother's side has applied for the position of clerk in your ministry. So far I have been financially responsible for him, and it has been a burden on my shoulders. I hope you will help him to get the job."

Jedi muttered that he would see what he could do, and they left at last.

"*I am really in it up to my neck*," he thought miserably. Now he had to contend with, not one, but three blackmailers, and two of them had the power to arrest him whenever they pleased. He went upstairs and lay flat on his bed, belly down, his head in his hands, moaning and tossing from side to side. How he wished that he had never met Emma King! How he regretted going to the 'Sunday school' on that particular Saturday! Because of a stupid little girl whose life did not matter to anyone, not even to her thug of a boyfriend, he had been reduced to a groveling rat.

But after a while, he thought, *Damn! This defeatism has to stop*. Was he not Jedidiah Thomas, OR, Permanent Secretary,

People's Warden, et cetera, et cetera? Surely, he should be able to squash a worm like Abdul with the heel of his shoe. A few words in the right quarters ought to be able to bring all the terrors of the earth crashing down on his filthy head. Yes, he should rouse himself from his lethargy and talk to someone. However, no sooner did the thought enter his head, than he realized that if he mentioned his problem to anyone, he would have to explain why Abdul was blackmailing him, which meant he would have to talk about the murder. And the moment he mentioned the murder to anyone he would be done for. Could he not simply appeal to Abdul's humanity? Abdul was a vicious thug; he had no human feelings. If he begged for mercy there would be no limit to the torture Abdul would inflict on him.

For three hours, Jedi lay on his bed trying to solve this conundrum, but he finally had to admit that there seemed to be no answer.

CHAPTER 8

At about six o'clock that evening, Jedi thought he should at least wash off the sweat and grease that had accumulated on his face. Normally, this was the time of day when he would start thinking about his evening meal, but he had no appetite and did not feel like doing anything. He had hardly stepped into the bathroom and turned on the tap when the front door bell rang, startling him again. *So this is my situation now*, he said to himself, sighing. *Any ringing sound sends me reeling.* Who could it be? Surely, not the police again! Should he pretend that he was not home? But his car was in the garage. The person must have seen it. He might even have heard the sounds coming from the bathroom. It might be a neighbor, a relative, or someone from the church. Was he in any mood for small talk after what he had been through that afternoon? In the end he decided that talking to someone other than one of Abdul's cabal would do him good, so he shouted, "coming!" and went downstairs to open the door.

"Ah, Mr. Thomas, it is so good to see you again."

The devil incarnate stood there, looking every inch the gigolo in the latest style in designer sneakers imported from the United States; a fawn, elegantly cut jacket with pleats on the pockets; impeccably pressed white gabardine trousers; and a white shirt with frills all down the front. His naturally curly hair shone with grease. Anyone who saw him would think that he was going to meet a girl friend rather than to indulge in sordid blackmail. The boy certainly had a nerve.

"Mr. Thomas, you are not being very polite," Abdul said more aggressively. "Never mind. I'll invite myself in." With that he strode past Jedi and once again ensconced himself in the best armchair.

Perhaps it was the irritation caused by Abdul's smug confidence and slick appearance, or perhaps it was a return of his recent determination to be tough with this insignificant piece of trash. Whatever the reason, Jedi stalked up to Abdul, and towered over him, yelling,

"Get out of my house at once, you filthy thief, you dog! What right do you have to stride into my lounge as though you were there when I was struggling to build this house? If you do not get out this instant I shall thrash you to within an inch of your life."

Jedi was himself surprised at the way his anger bubbled over. *This is good!*, he thought.

But Abdul was not to be browbeaten. Raising his voice in his turn, he said,

"Mr. Thomas, we both know the terrible things you have done to young people inside this very house, but if you think I am some silly ignorant girl that you can rape and then silence you are mistaken."

Jedi was quite alarmed by Abdul's counterattack, particularly since he knew that the neighbors, especially that busybody, Mama Sawyerr, must be listening. However, having realized that any sign of timidity only made the young beast more savage, he abandoned caution and shouted back,

"You dare to come to my house again to demand money after sending those two corrupt policemen here this afternoon?"

Abdul's demeanor changed abruptly and his surprise seemed genuine as he asked,

"Which policemen?"

"How do you mean which policemen? I mean constables Demoh and Bayoh.

I gave them two million five hundred thousand leones this afternoon which you have no doubt divided up among yourselves, and you still dare to come for more. Well, this time you will get nothing out of me."

"Mr. Thomas, calm down," Abdul said. "You know what policemen are like. I never sent Constables Bayoh and Demoh to you. They came of their own accord. And like a fool, you fell for their tricks. They will be in some bar right now, laughing at your stupidity and beginning to enjoy your two and a half million leones of which I am sure I will not see one cent. *I* am the offended party and you have given me nothing since you came back. Well, I want my own present from England and you are not going to get away with anything less than the two and a half million you gave to Demoh and Bayoh. I know you are loaded."

At this point, Jedi felt totally confused. Could it be that Abdul honestly did not know of the policemen's visit and the two and a half million they had extorted from him? If so, he was really in a mess. He had given two and a half million leones to the wrong people and Abdul would be relentless in demanding his own 'present.' Unless he sold his house or some other asset, he did not have that kind of money to give to him. In desperation, he bellowed.

"Do what you want! I don't have another cent to give you. And just get out of my house. Get out!"

"Or else?" Abdul sneered. "You will call the police? Go ahead! Call them. I am sure they will be delighted to learn about your criminal activities here. Go on, call the police!"

But Jedi was equally determined not to be browbeaten since he had no more money to give and really wanted Abdul out of his house.

"Get out of my house this minute," he said, his voice lower but even more intimidating.

Abdul took the wind right out of Jedi's sails by leaving the house at once. But as he walked down the street to the intersection, he kept turning to shout accusations at the top of his voice,

"I shall tell everyone about your filthy actions, Mr. Thomas. I shall let your minister know that you have no morals. I shall let all the workers at your office know that their boss is a criminal, that he is a man who corrupts young people, including schoolgirls. I shall let the whole world know. Just you wait! You will regret that you asked me out of your house. You will pay!"

Jedi looked on helplessly as Abdul made sure that every neighbor watching the scene heard his accusations. He realized that Abdul had decided to start a new phase in their relations: the phase of insinuating all kinds of suspicions about him into the minds of people who had always regarded him as a God-fearing man and a model of respectability. Abdul had announced to the world that he was guilty of horrible, corrupt, and immoral practices. How could he face his neighbors in the morning? That busybody, Mama Sawyerr, was bound to poke her gray head through her over-washed curtains when she saw his car going by and call out, "Good morning, Mr. Thomas" not out of good neighborliness, but to see whether his face registered any embarrassment, or shame. Others would be laughing at him behind their curtains, urging their husbands or wives to come and look at the secret malefactor. They would soon spread the word to colleagues in their offices, to the friends they met in the streets or the markets or at meetings of the Mothers Union, or the associations of Society Stewards or Wardens. The phones would soon be buzzing with stories and rumors about him, many of them distorted from the truth.

Jedi was horrified when he contemplated what people might now be thinking about him. In his ranting, Abdul had hinted that he was some sort of pervert, and a molester of young girls, but he had been careful not to come out with accusations of murder although his statements had left that possibility open. Abdul! He was so devilishly clever and calculating about everything he did. He obviously did not want to accuse him of murder because he had not finished milking him. For the moment, blackmail was his main objective.

Indeed Jedi began to regret antagonizing Abdul. Perhaps he should have been more accommodating. The consequence of his aggressiveness was that all his neighbors must now have a very unfavorable opinion of him. On further reflection, however, he was sure he had acted wisely. Abdul was not someone with whom one could come to an accommodation. After all, he had tried that before. No! He would continue to let him know in no uncertain terms that he would not get another cent. And if necessary, he would pursue the idea of hiring thugs to beat him up. He had been too soft with Abdul. From now on he would realize that he had disturbed a sleeping giant who was now wide awake and would squash him like the cockroach that he was. That was the way to handle him. Buoyed up by his resolve, Jedi spent the rest of the evening feeling relatively calm. He watched a video, ate some dinner, and went to bed. Next day he went to work as usual. He was surprised when he did not hear from Abdul for about two months after that.

It was towards the end of the second month that Mrs. Cole, came into his office to remind him that the following Friday he was due to be the guest speaker at the Speech Day and Prize-giving Ceremony of her alma mater, the Kennedy Preparatory School. It was she who had suggested his name to the principal who was also a member of their church's Mothers Union.

"Of course," Jedi said smoothly though uncharacteristically; he had forgotten all about it. "I shall certainly not disappoint you. These are some of the duties citizens in our position have to perform. It is a way of giving back to the community."

Like every other secondary school in Freetown, the Kennedy Preparatory School observed an annual speech day and prize-giving ceremony, but It was widely regarded as one of the worst schools in the area, its catchment group consisting of the rejects from other schools: girls so poor academically that they had no hope of being admitted to other schools, and the daughters of artisans and traders. There was a high drop-out and pregnancy rate among the pupils, though some of the alumnae, like Jedi's Mrs. Cole did defy the odds and make something of their lives. Jedi did not expect to enjoy the proceedings at such a third-rate school. They would no doubt consist of a pedestrian principal's report and mediocre gymnastic display and a badly-acted one-act play; but to be asked to be guest speaker at a speech day and prize-giving ceremony meant that one was numbered among the country's personages, so he worked on his speech assiduously, striving to make it simple yet uplifting.

Having secured such a distinguished guest speaker, the Kennedy Preparatory School was determined to make the most of the honor, so the coming speech day featured in the public announcements on the radio twice a day. Jedi basked in the glory of having his name, position and decoration broadcast on the radio so often. Mama Sawyerr and others could think what they liked. As far as the rest of the country was concerned, Jedidiah Thomas was an eminent personality, worthy of respect. In his state of euphoria, Jedi had put Abdul and any threat he might pose entirely out of his mind. People like that thug were basically bullies and therefore cowards, he thought, feeling smug. Cringe before them and they treated you like dirt and tried to grind you into the dust; but stand up to them and they drew back like the cowards they were. Violence, force, and the exercise of power were the only language they understood. His forcefulness during their previous encounter had probably paid off.

On the day of the prize-giving Jedi arrived at the school fifteen minutes before the ceremony was due to start. The Principal, resplendent in her academic robes, greeted him herself and led him to her office where they relaxed for a while over cake and lemon squash. Jedi had on his best British pin-striped suit, a brilliant white shirt, and his university tie, held in place by a gold tie-pin. A dark, three-piece, woolen suit was hardly appropriate in West Africa's ninety-degree heat, and Jedi knew he would probably be mopping his brow all afternoon. But that was all right. Distinguished men were expected to mop their brows.

On the stroke of four, the platform party, as the occasion's most distinguished people were called, made their way down the central aisle of the arena that had been specially constructed. The party consisted of members of the Board of Governors; the Deputy Minister of Education, representing the Honorable Minister of Education; the Principal Education Officer for Secondary Schools, representing the Chief Education Officer; the Principal; and the Distinguished Guest Speaker, Mr. Jedidiah Thomas, B. Sc, OR, Permanent Secretary. The entire audience rose as, accompanied by a suitable march blaring from a stereo system, the prestigious party made its way down the central aisle and through the admiring throng of parents, guardians, and well-wishers. Jedi held his head and shoulders high as the Principal showed him to his seat next to hers in the front row. The ceremony then began.

Jedi did his best to enjoy the items that the conscientious Principal, faculty and students of the Kennedy

Preparatory had prepared for their entertainment that afternoon. There was a more than mediocre gymnastic display by the Physical Education section in which a fat girl of about sixteen underestimated her weight and overestimated her ability and, in trying to leap over a vaulting horse, missed her step and crash-landed onto the floor of the stage to the tremendous enjoyment of her fellow students. There was a short sketch by the French club, which partly consisted of a family eating dinner. Their French, however, was incomprehensible even to those who knew some French, and some wags in the crowd, which was hardly from the best strata of society, shouted advice to them to the effect that if they tried not to speak with their mouths full they might be more intelligible. There was a play by the Drama club that lasted for the best part of an hour. The subject was interesting enough, but whoever put it together had no conception of plot and structure or character development or the proper use of language and style. It was about three girls of about sixteen or seventeen. One kept on advising the central figure to pay attention to her books and avoid boys. That way she would avoid becoming pregnant and dropping out of school and might well succeed in achieving her ambitions. She was a kind of good angel. The other, who was obviously the bad angel, gave the central figure some blatantly salacious advice on how to attract, not just boys, but men, much older men, men who worked in offices and for well-known companies and had wives and children at home, but also liked the company of young girls from time to time and had enough money to spend on them. Jedi was shocked. How could the school dare to stage a play like this during Speech Day? The bad angel was actually advising the central figure how to wiggle her hips, how to walk seductively, what to do with her eyes and her lips in order to get the men to pant after her like dogs on heat. The club even dared to bring a pregnant adolescent onto the stage. Perhaps the play was very much in line with the Principal's vision that included instilling into the girls a sense of self-respect and a determination to press on with their studies and not to be diverted by the temptations of the flesh, but it still seemed to Jedi to be in rather poor taste. To talk of such things was one thing; to represent them on the stage was quite another. However, the audience loved it. They shouted advice to the central figure. They whistled when the bad angel tried to teach her the art of wiggling her hips. They cheered and went into contortions of laughter when the pregnant adolescent appeared on stage and they were very forthcoming with suggestions as to how she got into that state. The laughter was largely caused by the fact that whoever did the costuming made a pretty bad job of it. The girl should have worn a loose fitting gown, but she was wearing a normal fairly tight dress, and the "pregnancy" was created by several pieces of linen amateurishly stuffed under the dress. She looked malformed rather than pregnant.

Jedi felt extremely uneasy as he waited to deliver his speech, partly because of the play, but more because, as he had been about to take his seat on the front row he had cast a condescending look all round him, and found himself staring straight into the eyes of – oh, horror of horrors - Abdul Sanusi. He was standing by the wall and Jedi now truly believed a statement he had often heard: that evil can look most attractive when it chooses to, for the young thug was smiling radiantly at him.

No one seeing Abdul that afternoon would have believed that he was a sadistic thug who had terrorized Jedi, extorted huge sums of money from him and tried to reduce him to abject impotence. What was he doing here? From the little Jedi knew about him, Abdul was the last person to be interested in a school's speech day. But then it occurred to Jedi that a young irresponsible like Abdul might feel that a school like Kennedy Prep was a fertile breeding ground for girls he wished to seduce. Perhaps that was why he had come: to size up the prey and take his pick among them. No wonder he was dressed so elegantly, *at my expense*, Jedi thought bitterly. Maybe his present girl friend, one of his present girl friends, or several of his present girl friends were currently enrolled at the school. It was quite possible. However, even after the ceremony had got well under way, Jedi felt Abdul's eyes upon him. Only then did it occur to him that the young thug had come, not to support a girl friend or check out new possibilities, but to torment him or worse. He must have heard those announcements on the radio and had come intending to degrade and expose him. This thought caused Jedi's heart to miss at least five beats. Sweat broke out all over his face and he really needed to mop his brow. Here he was, the most distinguished person in this august assembly, chosen to impart words of wisdom to the girls because of his achievements and moral qualities, and he was being confronted by an individual who could reduce him to nothingness in a minute if he wanted to.

In the intervals between items on the program of entertainment, Jedi had brief chats with the Principal. She said something that made him look to the right, and as he did so, he saw Abdul walking towards the front row. Did the arrogant boy not know that at such events it simply was not the done thing to talk to anyone sitting in the front row? Not even parents, relatives or better-appointed members of the audience would dare to do that. And yet, here was Abdul Sanusi walking straight up to the platform party. Deeply frightened all of a sudden, Jedi thought, *Is he coming to threaten me? Or to expose me? Is he coming to make his extortionate demands in the presence of the Principal, the Deputy Minister and the Principal Education Officer?* The Principal noticed his discomfort and was about to ask the young man to go back, when Abdul astonished them by affably offering his hand to Jedi with a bow.

"Good afternoon, Mr. Thomas, sir!" he said. "I am so delighted that you have honored the school with your august presence. I am looking forward to your speech, sir. I'm sure it will be full of advice that will benefit the girls. Thank you in advance, sir."

Looking the very picture of humility, respect and admiration for age and seniority, Abdul then greeted every member of the platform party. The other members of the front row were completely taken in by his charm. Even the Principal, who disapproved of his behavior, muttered as he withdrew,

"At least he knows how to show deference and respect to age, position, and achievement, which is much more than can be said for most young people nowadays." Jedi made no comment and she did not observe him shaking his head in disbelief.

Abdul walked back to his position by the wall and the events of the day continued. But Jedi could not forget his malign presence from then on. During the play, his comments were the loudest and some of them were obviously directed at Jedi. When the central character scorned the advice being given by the good angel Abdul shouted, "Leave her alone. Don't waste your advice on her. The chicken that does not hear 'sh' will hear the stone. The men will teach her a lesson."

After the entertainment, the entire front row moved on to the platform where seats were arranged for them. Jedi and the Principal were right in the center. The Principal then gave her report, which was loudly applauded. The loudest applause came from Abdul who never took his eyes off Jedi. As he waited on tenterhooks to deliver his speech, Jedi started wondering what Abdul planned to do. After the Principal's report, the next item was not the Guest Speaker's speech, but the distribution of prizes, and that seemed to go on forever. By the time they came to his speech it was getting dark. Some members of the audience were becoming restless. Jedi even heard someone mutter, "It is about time we went home. What more is there to be said?"

At last it was his turn, but before he began to speak he had to be formally introduced by the Chairman of the Board of Governors who praised him to the skies as a man of the highest integrity in a society where there was so much corruption. He mentioned Jedi's academic achievements, his perseverance as a young boy and a student in a foreign country, his distinguished record in the civil service, his contribution to the development of the country, his record of voluntary service, his Christian principles and his service to his church and his God. He was indeed a pillar of the community, and they could not have asked for a better Guest Speaker. The chairman's comments were interrupted by tremendous applause, Abdul's being the loudest.

Eventually, Jedi was invited to deliver his speech. There was a similarity between the message of the play and the one he had prepared. He knew that the forward-looking new Principal was anxious to inspire these young girls to avoid distractions, concentrate on their studies and confound the predictions of those who thought they were doomed to failure. He knew that one of the most troubling problems at the school was the early dropouts due to teenage pregnancy. So he had written a speech that would reinforce the Principal's concerns and vision. He had prepared and waited several weeks to give this speech, but now that the big moment arrived he found himself feeling nervous, even terrified, and all because of that demon, Abdul. As he walked up to the podium he could not help glancing in Abdul's direction. To his surprise, Abdul was no longer there. Had he gone away because he felt he had done enough damage and had embarrassed him enough for one day? Jedi certainly hoped so.

The speech started well enough. Jedi had a clear, resonant, compelling bass voice that would have carried right though to all sections of the audience, even without the help of a microphone. He knew he had the audience under his thumb and after the preliminary thanks, congratulations, and jokes, he settled down to the meat of his message.

Then a strange thing happened. Right out of nowhere another booming voice came through what sounded like a competing microphone, or rather, megaphone. The audience became distracted, and the other members of the platform party looked aghast. The Principal craned her elegant neck to see what was going on and signaled to one of her faculty to go and investigate. Visibly shaken and taken aback, Jedi looked to the Principal for some guidance as to what he should do. What was even more disturbing were the words coming through this competing megaphone. When Jedi, in trying to motivate the girls, declared that he himself had been driven in his own career by a sense of purpose and sheer industry, the voice boomed, "Yes, girls, listen to Mr. Jedidiah Thomas, the Permanent Secretary. His purpose includes going to Sunday school on Saturday and Sunday afternoons to look for young school girls to seduce."

The interest of the audience had now been kindled, but not in Jedi's speech. One individual shouted, "Aha, truth is coming out. Let us listen."

The consternation on the faces of the members of the platform party was unmistakable. Jedi's expression suggested a desperate desire for the ground to open beneath his feet and swallow him up. How on earth had Abdul contrived it? What should he do now? He had to do something; otherwise, his disgrace would be complete. He could no longer look the Principal in the eye, and decided that the best thing would be to compete with the voice from the megaphone; drown it out. At least, ensure that there was so much confusion from the competing voices that the audience would not be able to make out anything. So he went on with the speech, shouting out the prepared statement that he hoped the example of his own life would inspire the girls to reach for higher heights. But the voice would not be drowned, and responded to that statement by saying,

"That's right, my dear girls. Let Mr. Thomas inspire you and teach you how to lose your virtue and your honor. He is an expert on such things. Go to Sunday School and let him take you to his house and his bed on Juba Hill."

The voice was proving more successful because of its superior technique. Instead of trying to drown Jedi out, it let him go on and make specific moral statements which were clearly heard by the crowd, then interrupted to expose Jedi's hypocrisy. The audience listened with glee. This was proving more entertaining than they had expected. Even those who had started to leave, returned and hoped the show would continue. And it continued as long as Jedi went on with his speech. Apart from the platform party, the audience was delighted, for there is nothing a Freetown crowd loves better than scandal. One member remarked,

"A big breeze is blowing; a big tree is about to fall."

Another chimed in,

"Who would have expected such a thing of a Permanent Secretary, an elder of the church at that?"

"But they are all doing it," a young woman interjected. "That is their constant employment. They even do it in their offices."

Sweating profusely, Jedi soldiered on, urging the girls to keep their purpose clearly in focus and resist temptations of all kinds, particularly in these days of moral delinquency when the temptations of money and pleasure were all around them.

"Yes, sir!" boomed the voice. "You can say that again. And Mr. Jedidiah Thomas knows all about such things. He knows about tempting schoolgirls with his Mercedes Benz, his Permanent Secretary's salary, the pleasures of his house on

Juba Hill and his air-conditioned office. Why don't you check out his place, girls? You can even go there in your school uniforms. He has good medical contacts, so that if there are any problems he can take care of business."

And so the contest between the two voices went on, the voice from the megaphone counterpointing Jedi's and revealing his perversions, immorality, hypocrisy, and secret vices for all to hear. Jedi could simply have stopped, but to have done so would have been to hand a clear victory to Abdul and concede that the accusations were true. So he rushed through the rest of the speech mechanically, omitting several significant passages. When he finished, there was polite clapping from the platform party, but jeers and roars of laughter from the audience who shouted, "More, more, more." Only the more they wanted was from the megaphone voice, not from Jedi.

Scandalized, the Principal hurriedly rose to thank Jedi for his inspiring speech and brought the ceremony to a close. What she had hoped would be a glorious, uplifting ceremony had turned out to be an unmitigated disaster. Mrs. Cole, who had been looking forward to going up to her Permanent Secretary to congratulate him on the speech, thank him for coming, and bask in his reflected glory, could not bear to face him or the Principal. She slunk away as quickly as she could without talking to anyone. The members of the Board disappeared just as quickly to avoid having to make excuses for refusing an invitation to the Principal's office for refreshments. In any case, they doubted that this would take place now. As for Jedi, he could not bear to look at anybody. He muttered a hasty goodbye to the Principal and walked quickly to his car, aware of the ribald comments directed at him as he passed. The crowd was enormous and cars had to move slowly to reach the main road, which gave people ample opportunity to throw more ribald comments at his car as he moved off with the windows wound up and the locks down. Afterwards, he really could not remember how he managed to get home to his refuge on Juba Hill.

CHAPTER 9

Jedi was aware that for the next few days he was virtually the talk of the town. The debacle at the Kennedy Preparatory School was not exactly mentioned in the press or on radio or television, but it was widely reported in the real popular press, the press of mouth-to-mouth and person-to-person communication. Various people told their own version of the story of the top civil servant who laid snares for young girls at 'Sunday Schools', and seduced them in his office or at his house. Many people sympathized with Jedi, however, saying it was a common practice, and that it was only this particular civil servant's misfortune to be exposed. The fertile imaginations of gossips were at their most fevered. Jedi was reported to have been seen at several haunts he could never possibly have visited and to have made passes at people who had never come within hundreds of yards of him. Old Mama Sawyerr told her friends and acquaintances at the Mothers' Union that she had seen Jedi "ferry" several young women at ungodly hours of the day and night to his hideout on Juba Hill. How could he pretend to be such an upright God-fearing man while engaging in such immoral activities? What a hypocrite! There were several days for the thief, she said, but there would be one day for the master of the house. God, the master of the house, had set his trap and exposed Jedi's evil doings.

"I knew that something was brewing," Ethan Spencer told Elkanah Pratt when the scandal was reported to them at a meeting of the Sidesmen and Sideswomen's Union which Jedi did not attend. "I knew there was something behind all those strange phone calls. An intelligent and astute man like Jedi Thomas! How did he manage to get caught?"

"He overdid it," opined Elkanah. "He went too far, or he made it too obvious. He thought that because of his position no one would dare to expose him, particularly in public. These days one has to be so careful. I wouldn't be in the least surprised if the whole thing was contrived by someone in his office who wants to bring him down and take over his position. That kind of thing is constantly happening in the civil service."

"I am sorry for him, "said Ethan. "I doubt whether he can now become Grand Master of his Masonic lodge. And I don't think there is the slightest chance of his being re-elected People's Warden. That should create a great opening and opportunity for you, Elkanah."

"Well," Elkanah demurred, "let's not count my chickens as yet; let's wait and see."

Jedi could not face his office for the next few days, and when he did go, he could scarcely look at Mrs. Cole, and she pointedly avoided his eyes. During those few days, their relationship was perfunctory and official. The Principal had blamed Mrs. Cole for suggesting as guest speaker someone of such dubious character when she wanted someone in whose glory the school would bask, who would give emphasis to her new vision. Look at what she had got!

Jedi knew that he was the subject of conversation in all the corridors of the ministry and during the lunch and coffee breaks. That devil Abdul's revenge had been enormously successful. He had clearly demonstrated that he could smash Jedi if the latter tried to thwart him. And he was clever enough to do it, Jedi conceded. On the evening of the fiasco at the Kennedy Preparatory Abdul had called to say that he hoped Jedi now realized that it was almost suicidal to annoy him, that he hoped Jedi would now give him his own present from

England. Jedi had been forced to borrow money from here and there to put together the two and a half million leones Abdul demanded. And he was sure that that would not be Abdul's last demand. He remembered that during the fiasco at the Kennedy Preparatory the voice from the megaphone had not mentioned murder. So Abdul was still keeping that in reserve. Jedi realized that he was now in an impossible position. He hardly spoke to his colleagues outside official business, scarcely attended church meetings, missed church services and even failed to turn up for meetings of his Masonic lodge. What could he do? Compared to his present situation, his vacation in the United Kingdom had been an idyll. He had rested, slept, eaten his fill, watched television and gone to the movies. Thinking about the movies made Jedi suddenly remember the one in which the blackmailer had been brutally murdered by his victim. That had to be the answer. This problem would not go away as long as both he and Abdul remained on the surface of the earth; one of them had to go.

So it was that the idea of killing Abdul slowly took shape in Jedi's mind. He had heard someone say, maybe it was even in that movie, that all blackmailers were asking to be murdered because a blackmailer was always a callous individual with a thief's mentality. Having realized he was on to a good thing, he would never willingly stop bleeding the victim. Murder was the only answer.

Murder! Jedi shuddered at the thought. Could he really bring himself to commit a murder? Cold-blooded murder was something that Europeans and Americans did, not Africans. Cold-blooded murder was not part of his culture. Besides, he was a God-fearing, church-going Christian who had frequently heard the commandment "Thou shalt do no murder". It then occurred to him that the way Africans got rid of their enemies could hardly be called murder because they seldom did it themselves using knives or guns or poison. Africans killed their enemies indirectly, through juju or witchcraft: African science, as some would call it! In most cases, there would be no contact between the killer and his enemy. No one would see him do it; or see anyone do it for that matter; and there would be no clues. The victim would simply sicken and die or collapse and die, or he might die in a fire or an accident or in a flood, or by drowning. For all practical purposes he would seem to die of natural causes or in an accident or in a natural disaster. Surely, Jedi thought, this could not be what was meant by murder. It was subtle and sophisticated, not brutal and bold-faced as it was in the West; it could hardly be called murder. He could think of several examples of people in Freetown who had probably been killed by their enemies in this way, yet no one could point a finger at a killer because no one person could be linked to the death. That was how it was done in Africa.

Thus, Jedi's warped thinking led him honestly to believe that he could enlist the services of a medicine man to kill Abdul and still not be guilty of murder. Being an intelligent, thinking man, he also wrestled intellectually and philosophically with the issues attendant on using the services of a medicine man. How, for instance, could he reconcile what he was planning with his Christian beliefs? The belief that malevolent spirits could be harnessed in the service of man was part of traditional African religion but was hardly countenanced by Christianity, or even Islam for that matter. He knew that there were thousands of Christians, who would be indignant if their Christian faith were called into question, who regularly went to church on Sundays, worshipped their maker and were leaders or members of several Christian organizations, who even read their Bibles regularly, but who would not hesitate to consult a medicine man and use African juju when they found themselves in a jam. Christianity was fine when all was well, but in an emergency, it had to be the medicine man. He even knew some scientists at the university, who declared such beliefs and practices to be contrary to the scientific attitude and world-view, but who would nevertheless consult medicine men to advance their careers or their fortunes. And as for politicians! They did it all the time. Medicine men made most of their money during elections. There were even some ministers of religion who had been known to place their faith in medicine men. If clergymen saw no contradiction between that and their Christian faith, why should he?

So Jedi had rationalized and justified his decision to use African juju to get rid of his arch-enemy. He made discreet inquiries about the most efficient medicine men in the Freetown area. One had to be careful. He had heard that there were lots of quacks who charged enormous fees without any results yet, for obvious reasons, were never publicly accused of fraud or incompetence. He started by asking the messengers and cleaners apparently casual questions and discovered that they were well informed about medicine men and did not raise their eyebrows over a senior civil servant who might need their services. To them, consulting medicine men was a routine event.

One dark evening Jedi found himself picking his way among the rocks and dirt of a back street in the so-called Akaymori area in the south end of Freetown, towards the home of one Pa Kelfala. Since no one should recognize him while he was on this secret and deadly mission, he had decided to go at night. He parked his car some distance away, not even along Mountain Cut, which would have been most convenient, but along Regent Road, and he walked the considerable distance to Pa Kelfala's place. As he had done on the night of his rendezvous with Abdul at King Jimmy, he had disguised himself by wearing some of his oldest and shabbiest clothes and an old cloth cap which he brought well down over his eyes so that his face could hardly be seen. As he walked towards Pa Kelfala's hideout that night, he wondered at the depths to which Abdul had made him sink. Never mind! He told himself. He would soon be rid of him. He would wipe him completely off the face of the earth and ensure that he never troubled decent people again.

Pa Kelfala's part of the city was one of the poorest in Freetown. The street, if one could call it that, inclined steeply toward a hilly area. All the houses were shabby and dilapidated: shacks rather than houses. Most of them had been constructed with old corrugated iron sheets, bush sticks, and whatever materials came to hand. The sheets that formed the roofs of the houses had to be kept in place and prevented from being blown away by big rocks and a few concrete blocks. There were few windows, all made of wood, and it was obvious that some of the houses had no bathrooms, certain places behind the buildings or even parts of the street being used for that purpose. The protruding stomachs of the children still roaming around proclaimed their malnutrition. Only the deadly purpose on which he was bent could have brought Jedi to this epitome of squalor. Pa Kelfala had a great reputation and must be making quite a decent living, so Jedi wondered why he chose to stay in such a place, thus forcing his well-heeled clients to associate with filth if they wanted his services. Could it be in the nature of medicine men to live in the poorest areas?

This was his second trip to Pa Kelfala's house. On his first visit, he had been surprised at the old man's shrunken, wizened and shabby appearance. The room into which he ushered Jedi was almost dark: lit only by a small tin kerosene lamp with a   wick. At one end of the room stood Pa Kelfala's shabby bed, and all kinds of objects and utensils lined the other three walls. It was clear that the one window was never opened, which explained the room's distinctly musty smell.

How incongruous, Jedi thought, that a so-called medicine man lived in such unhealthy surroundings.

Pa Kelfala gave him a low stool to sit on. He had started to tell the old man his problem, when he cut him short, saying,

"Wait. *I* will tell you."

Pa Kelfala drew from a brown cloth bag several cowries and other strange objects which he mixed with red and white kola nuts that had been split into segments. He shook the mixture together, muttering incantations, then tossed the lot on to the dirt floor.

"There!" he said. "You have an enemy and you want me to kill him."

"These objects and my spirits have told me," Pa Kelfala said, seeing Jedi's look of utter amazement."

That answer dispelled all of Jedi's lingering doubts that he had made a good choice of medicine man. He now burst into tears, having heard that weeping helped to convince a medicine man that your enemy deserved to be killed. After all, killing a human being was a serious matter. Most medicine men, so he had been told, refused to do it unless they were absolutely convinced that you were the aggrieved party. So Jedi's tears flowed copiously as he said,

"It is a young man, sir. He has disgraced me and is determined to continue disgracing me until he destroys or even kills me. And he has already taken a huge amount of money from me; in fact, all my savings. You are my last hope, sir."

Jedi did not give further details, nor did Pa Kelfala require any more. He merely said, "These young men of today! When will they realize that they are asking for trouble when they decide to disgrace big men?"

"This one has made me the laughing stock of my office, my church, and my neighborhood," Jedi went on. "And he is enjoying my disgrace."

"That is bad," Pa Kelfala agreed. "But before I proceed, I have to be sure that your heart is clean, that you have not offended him or anyone related to him, and that it is he who has offended you. If your heart is not clean, what I do may not take effect."

Jedi swore that his heart was quite clean and that he had not offended the young man in any way.

"Then we will proceed," Pa Kelfala said, at which Jedi rejoiced, thinking, *Abdul, you are as good as dead.*

At Pa Kelfala's request, he then went on to describe Abdul in detail to give the old man some idea of his appearance, personality and character. Pa Kelfala had then told Jedi that his fees included the cost of a big white cock, some rice, kola nuts, and various other items that he would procure against Jedi's second visit when the deed would be done.

It was for this second visit that Jedi was now making his way to Pa Kelfala's house. In the divination room, Pa Kelfala showed him the items he had bought, including the big white cock that lay bound in one corner. Jedi handed over the rest of the fees and the procedure began. Bringing out his cowries and other tools of his trade, Pa Kelfala muttered long incantations, threw the objects on the floor and observed their configuration. He rearranged them, picked them up, shook them together and threw them down again, all the while muttering incantations. At times he raised his eyes to the ceiling as though invoking some spirit lodged there; at times he gazed at the floor. At times he spread his palms open and turned them upwards; at times he clenched them into fists. Then he rose, went to one corner of the room, and brought out a calabash that was covered by another. Both calabashes were decorated with cowries and bits of the thin red cloth known as 'tafti'. Sitting down once more, Pa Kelfala opened the calabash and took out an oblong mirror with a leather border. Its handle was six inches long.

"Come nearer," he said to Jedi, then launched into the most intense incantations of all. Suddenly he stopped and told Jedi to look into the mirror.

Jedi's jaw dropped, when he saw that a reflection not his own, had formed in the mirror. It was the handsome face of a young man and bore an uncanny resemblance to Abdul.

" Is that the person who has offended you, the young man you wish to kill?"

"Yes, sir!" Jedi replied, still shocked.

"You are absolutely sure?"

"Yes, sir."

"Very well."

Pa Kelfala then reached behind him and with some difficulty pulled out an object which consisted of a leather-wrapped piece of wood or iron, about nine inches long. Its round head was also wrapped in leather.

"Take this," he said, "and hit that face as hard as you can. Don't mind the mirror."

Jedi took the weapon, raised it high and, concentrating into the blow all the rage and hatred that Abdul had produced in him, brought it down with all his might. Miraculously the mirror did not crack, but the image reflected in it shattered and diffused into what looked like a mass of blood and flesh.

"Hit it again!" Pa Kelfala said, and Jedi complied again and again and again, expending all his pent-up resentment and energy in the exercise. When he stopped he was quite sure that Abdul was done for. Pa Kelfala then grabbed the cock and, with an expert slash of a knife, slit its throat, and let the blood flow on to the floor.

Now, we'll see who is master, Jedi thought triumphantly.

CHAPTER 10

It was once again the Christian season of Lent, a period of penitence during which the faithful fast, give up luxuries and indulgencies, and mortify themselves for their sins in preparation for the glorious feast of Easter. Right in the middle of Lent, after a spiritual lapse of some weeks, brought on by his intense humiliation at the Kennedy Preparatory School's speech day, Jedi resumed his religious observance and church duties. His decision to do so followed his trips to Pa Kelfala. He regarded them as successful, because after that vengeful smashing of Abdul's face and the shedding of the cock's blood, he had been absolutely sure that Abdul's days were numbered. He had felt it in his bones. At the moment when the weapon struck that deadly blow, his whole body had vibrated as if it possessed enough supernatural power to accomplish whatever he wanted it to do. And as the white cock emitted its last croak and its blood trickled freely on to the dirt floor, he had felt Abdul's satanic powers deserting him and his useless life ebbing into nothingness.

So when Jedi went to church one Sunday after that, it was with a confidence and vitality that had completely deserted him during the previous weeks. He felt he could now regard with scorn all those fellow church members who sought to avoid him or who greeted him hypocritically, concealing their derision and hatred beneath their smiles. He did not care two hoots for them. Who were they anyway? He had shown his mastery and his power by shedding the blood of a repulsive bully, by ridding the world of worthless vermin. The members of the congregation might have noticed something strange about Jedi's singing. His voice rang out more loudly than usual, and he sang the doleful Lenten hymns and the psalms, not with solemnity and remorse, but with a note of triumph. As he moved about with the other sidesmen to take up the offering during the singing of one of the hymns, members of the congregation might have noticed an extra bounce in his stride. He seemed happy, and they might well have asked themselves how that could be when he had been so badly humiliated and exposed recently. In fact, Jedi saw the hand of Providence operating throughout the church service. The offertory hymn was one of his favorites, and one that had been sung on an earlier occasion when he felt he had been providentially delivered from disaster, again miraculously, he thought, because then as now, he had had no part in the selection of the hymns. It seemed as if Providence Itself had inspired someone to select that most appropriate hymn, 'Through all the changing scenes of life, in trouble and in joy...' Once again, he was particularly struck by that reassuring verse:

The hosts of God encamp around
The dwellings of the just;
Deliverance he affords to all
Who on his succor trust.

The first time it happened, it was when he felt he had reached the nadir of his fortunes, when it seemed that Abdul, the demon, had almost absolute power over him. God had come to his aid, encamped around his dwelling and brought him deliverance because he was just and trusting. God had inspired and invigorated him and given him the power to pound his enemy's face to smithereens, and spill his venomous blood. Yes, God was good! Alleluia!

Two weeks later, it was Easter Sunday. The atmosphere suited Jedi's mood even more, for the whole church was decorated with flowers and buntings in happy celebration of Christ's glorious resurrection and triumph over the forces of Satan, sin, death, and hell. Jedi felt that he, too, had triumphed over the satanic forces of evil that had sought to destroy him. He, like Christ, could be said to have trodden the forces of Satan underfoot and to hold the keys of death. Hadn't he contrived and accomplished the death of his arch-enemy? So he sang the Easter hymns with as much joy and fervor as though they had been written for specifically for him:

> The strife is o'er, the battle done;
> The victory of life is won;
> The song of triumph has begun;
> Alleluia!

The glorious Easter service was followed by further celebration and feasting at the home of one of the sidesmen. Jedi did not care what some of them might be thinking of him. He joined in the bonhomie and the revelry, and enjoyed himself fully, before going home to Juba Hill to sleep out the rest of a triumphant day.

It did not occur to him that his victory celebration might be premature, for he saw a combination of circumstances pointing surely to Abdul's demise. Apart from the amazing and dramatic happenings at Pa Kelfala's house, there was the peculiar coincidence of that offertory hymn during Lent, and the one on Easter Sunday. Abdul must be dying by now. He expected to hear the news any day though he knew of no one he could contact to find out whether indeed, that dog, had died. He was just sure that when it happened he would know it, somehow. His conviction was strengthened, when, for a period of about three months after Easter, he heard nothing from Abdul. The dog must surely be dead. He had dared to trifle with an elephant and had been trodden under a majestic and terrible foot. From now on, Jedi expected to live out his life in peace. His circumstances had been considerably reduced, but he could start rebuilding; he had the energy, determination, and vision to succeed. In another year or so the Abdul episode would be nothing more than a bad dream. He was thankful that he had not discussed it with anyone, so there would be no one to remind him of that most despicable individual,

Picture Jedi's consternation and horror, then, when, on another Sunday afternoon, the ringing of his doorbell roused him from his usual nap, and he went down to open the door only to find Abdul standing at the threshold, looking the very picture of health, wealth, and contentment.

CHAPTER 11

"Mr. Thomas," Abdul said in high glee, "you look as though you have seen a ghost. Did you think I was dead?"

Jedi's expression did suggest that. Had he been a white person his terror and surprise would have shown in the bloodless pallor of his skin. As it was, his complexion was now a ghastly gray; his eyes stared, his mouth gaped, his brow glistened with sweat, and his hands and knees visibly shook.

Abdul swept past him into the lounge, saying,

"As usual, you don't have the courtesy to invite me in, so I shall walk in myself."

With that he ensconced himself in the most comfortable chair, swung an elegant leg over the arm, took out a cigarette, lit it, and started puffing away. Jedi had followed him inside and had sunk weakly into the nearest chair. As he continued to stare at Abdul, his expression gradually changed from horrified astonishment to deep aversion.

For a while Abdul ignored him and concentrated on looking at various objects in the room as though he owned them or would like to own them. When his gaze finally settled on Jedi, he noticed the expression of hatred and, feigning surprise, said, "Mr. Thomas, you look as though you would like to kill me."

You can say that again, thought Jedi who had begun to regain his composure.

"You have no right to be alive, you scum," he spat.

Abdul's comments had been strangely pointed and true, so Jedi could not be sure whether he was aware of the double meaning in that statement. Was he aware of the attempt to kill him? You could never tell with this demon. Not only was he resourceful, he now seemed to possess a kind of sixth sense.

Abdul said, chuckling, "Well, as you can see, I am very much alive and enjoying life, thanks to your stupidity and generosity."

Jedi let out an exasperated sigh.

"What do you want now? I have nothing more to give you; you know that."

"Mr. Thomas, I can never believe that a man in your position has no more money or cannot find some. Anyway, I have not come for money today; only to let you know that I am still alive, in case you had forgotten, and to assure you that you will never be rid of me as long as we are both alive. You and your possessions belong to me now, and I can come whenever I like to collect what is mine. Give me a beer."

Abdul's tone was insulting, but Jedi felt slightly relieved to hear that he had not come to demand more money, so he rose and brought him the beer without comment. He was alarmed by the implications of what Abdul had said, but he would deal with that later. It was quite obvious that Abdul was absolutely satisfied with the current situation. He drank in contented silence. Jedi watched him without saying anything.

Not long afterwards, Abdul departed. Jedi felt like a man whose reprieve from a death sentence had been overturned. Why was Abdul still alive? Pa Kelfala had assured him that Abdul would die, and Pa Kelfala had a solid reputation. If he could not get rid of Abdul with Pa Kelfala's assistance, could he ever get rid of him? He decided on another consultation.

Pa Kelfala muttered his incantations, threw his cowries and kola nuts on the floor, studied their configuration and sighed.

"You told me that your heart was clean and that you had not offended this young man or anyone connected with him."

"Yes, sir, that is true," Jedi lied again. "My heart is clean. I have never had an evil intention towards that boy and I have never offended him or any of his relations. In fact, I did not know him."

"Well, my objects tell me a different story. Anyway, I can only advise patience. If your heart is clean, as you say, be patient, and you will see what will happen. At times these things take time; but I warn you, your heart must be clean."

As Jedi drove back home, he remembered Pa Kelfala's warning. He knew that his heart was not clean, at least, not towards Abdul. He detested him wholeheartedly. How could he have said that his heart was clean? Was this why Pa Kelfala's art had not taken effect? Or had Pa Kelfala duped him by saying, "Your heart must be clean?" Perhaps he was guarding against possible failure. What could he do now?

During the next two months Abdul made Jedi's life as miserable as possible. He did not ask for more money, but took every opportunity to show Jedi that he was now his master. For instance, he went to the Juba Hill house one Saturday afternoon just after Jedi had finished his lunch. Juldeh answered the door, and was flabbergasted when, instead of asking whether the master was at home and whether he could see him, Abdul strolled confidently past him without saying a word and took the chair which his boss always used when he sat in the downstairs lounge. Juldeh stood by the door, dumbfounded that this useless vagabond had not even bothered to greet him before sweeping into his boss's lounge and installing himself in the best chair. What was the relationship between his boss and this boy?

"Don't just stand there like a fool!" Abdul shouted as he took out his cigarette and lit it. "Go and tell your master that Mr. Abdul is here, and bring me a beer."

Juldeh was livid with rage. Observing the pecking order was very important in a city like Freetown. Everyone sought to find someone to whom he was superior. Juldeh knew he was a steward and therefore inferior to his boss who paid his wages and was entitled to be called 'master.' In turn he carefully estimated the value of anyone who entered his master's compound and instinctively knew which ones were inferior to him. He had no doubt that this gangsterish young man was his inferior, despite his flashy clothes. That he should dare, therefore, to speak to him in that way and bark out orders was absolutely unbearable. So Juldeh said,

"Fellow! Who are you calling a fool? Don't think that because you are wearing fine clothes you can come to my boss's house and talk to me anyhow you like. I will not stand for it. Besides, I take orders only from him. So don't give me orders in this house."

"If I want to be your master, I can be your master, damn you!" Abdul replied. "I am your master's master. And if I am your master's master, I am your master. So don't give me any cheek. Just tell your master I am here and bring my beer if you want to keep your job."

From his upstairs bedroom Jedi heard the altercation between Abdul and Juldeh and rushed downstairs to put a stop to it. He knew that Juldeh could be hot-tempered, and that though he was usually pleasant enough, he could blaze into uncontrollable rage when offended. Moreover, he had a good deal of innate Fulani pride in him. His people had come down considerably in the world, and he was now forced to eke out his living in a strange land, but that did not mean that he was prepared to forget his proud descent from Fulani nobles and put up with any nonsense. Besides, Jedi knew that any prolonged confrontation between the two young men might reveal the true nature of his relationship with Abdul.

"Look here, Abdul," he yelled, "if you want to continue to be welcome in this house you will have to observe basic decency and courtesy and show some manners. This is a quiet neighborhood. I cannot have you coming here to disturb the peace. Whenever you come you must remain at the door until I give my steward the signal to let you in. That is how things are done in a civilized society."

"I have already told your high class neighbors about some of the uncivilized things that have gone on in this house," said Abdul, with a sneer. "I will now tell your stupid steward so that he can know what kind of a master he has."

Jedi cringed at the thought of Juldeh knowing his secret and hurriedly ordered him back to the kitchen, saying, "I will take care of this."

Though Juldeh was in a towering rage, his curiosity was stronger. Who was this young man? What hold did he have over his master that he could speak to him like that and even dare to give his servants orders? He wanted to find out, so he delayed going back to the kitchen and stood where he was, glaring as Abdul continued,

"No, I want him to stay and find out what kind of a master he has and what goes on in this house when darkness comes. Let me see whether he will respect you then."

Jedi had begun to sweat profusely. He could not afford to let Juldeh know his secret. Not only would he lose all respect for him, the whole world would get to know. In desperation, he bawled,

"Juldeh, didn't you hear me? I said, go back to the kitchen. *I* will handle this."

Juldeh took a couple of reluctant steps towards the kitchen.

"And he had better bring my beer without delay," Abdul proclaimed. Jedi could see that he was working himself up into a simulation of rage, so to pacify him, he said quietly,

"Juldeh, please bring him a beer."

Abdul began to breathe as heavily as if his chest were an oversized bellows. His face twitched, his eyes blazed. He looked almost majestic in his fake anger.

"Mr. Thomas, I have told you," he threatened after Juldeh had brought him the beer, "I am now your master, and you have to do as I say. If you don't, you know the consequences. You boy!" he yelled at Juldeh's receding figure, "let me tell you; if I want your master to lick my boots I can make him lick my boots. So you'd better not mess with me."

Abdul continued ranting at Jedi who signaled once more for Juldeh to go back to the kitchen.

"After I have done all I can to accommodate you and to help you! You know I have information that can destroy you if it were widely known. You plead with me to keep your secret, and I keep it; and this is the gratitude I get. You encourage your illiterate, stinking, 'woroko,' boy to insult me. I will not stand for it."

"Please, keep your voice down," Jedi pleaded, thoroughly demoralized and intimidated. After pretending to make a great effort to control his rage, Abdul said more calmly,

"Well, you must tell your boy that I am master here; that whenever I come here he must let me in without question and give me a beer and do whatever I say. In fact, you must tell him that I have the right to come here whenever I choose, at any hour of the day, and that whether or not you are at home, he must let me in."

Jedi knew that from his vantage point in the kitchen Juldeh was listening intently to all that was being said, and that the steward would consider it highly irregular to be told to let anyone into the house when his master was not in, let alone this gangster. How could he instruct Juldeh to let Abdul into the house at all hours? He felt he must take a stand, make some last resistance.

"How do you expect me to tell my steward to let you into the house whether or not I am at home? No one comes into this house when I am not in. How else can I protect myself against thieves?"

"So you are now giving your boy the impression that I am a thief", Abdul said, raising his voice again. "You are adding insult to injury and I will show you that there are certain things in this world that are worse than stealing. You and your boy will find that it would have been better if you had been a thief."

With that he rose, adding, "I can see there is no point arguing with you. I am going to the police."

Jedi dared not take the risk of assuming that he was merely bluffing.

"All right," he said, feeling sick. "I will tell him. You need not fear that there will be any further confrontation between the two of you."

So Jedi 'handled' that situation, but at what a price! He had cowered in front of Abdul in the presence of his steward. He had virtually acknowledged that Abdul was his master by agreeing to let his steward know that Abdul had the right to come into the house whenever he liked. Now Juldeh knew that Abdul had total hold on him and that he must have done something that would destroy him if it were known. He was sure that Juldeh would no longer respect him. Juldeh might even leave his service because he could not bear to be ordered around by a boy like Abdul. Stewards of single men were privileged people. They had no mistresses to order them around, and so were virtually the masters of the house when their bosses had gone off to work. It was a very pleasant existence. If Abdul made good his threat to come to the house even if Jedi was out, not only would he be in Juldeh's way, he would also behave as if he were master which would lead to further confrontation. And who could say what would happen then? Jedi realized that his dealings with Abdul had entered yet another phase: one in which his steward no longer respected him and knew that he had been involved in something despicable or even criminal. The situation was fraught with danger.

Jedi now became more and more depressed. He was sure that Juldeh had once regarded him as a stern, upright, disciplined man, someone to obey and respect. Would Juldeh continue to respect a man who seemed to be involved in shady and even criminal activities? Juldeh had also seen him cower in front of a mere boy and do as the boy wished. He had seen him lose his assertiveness, his air of command, and his confidence. Surely, Juldeh would think this was not a man to respect.

Jedi himself felt that he was losing his grip. He moped around the house, shuffling and dragging his feet instead of walking confidently and strongly, his head held high as he used to before; he paid less attention to his personal appearance and his personal hygiene. When he gave orders to Juldeh, he did so feebly, as though he did not expect to be obeyed, and he noticed that Juldeh no longer bothered to say, "Yes, sir." He even lost his assertiveness at the office and in his dealings with his fellow parishioners at meetings of the various church societies. He found out that he was forgetting things and becoming absent-minded. Once, when he went shopping, to his great embarrassment, he discovered that he had forgotten his wallet only when he wanted to pay for the goods he wished to buy. He knew he was deteriorating rapidly, and what was most distressing, that there seemed to be no solution to the problem.

Abdul made good his threat to go to the house when Jedi was not there. On one occasion, he apparently brought a friend with him, and they proceeded to eat and drink to their heart's content and at Jedi's expense. On another occasion Jedi arrived home from work to find Abdul already settled in his favorite chair, serenely smoking a cigarette, drinking a beer and dozing in between. Jedi was surprised to discover that relations between Abdul and Juldeh had changed remarkably. Looking at them, you would never believe that they had almost come to blows on an earlier occasion and seemed set to remain inveterate enemies. Their relationship seemed almost cordial now, so much so that when Abdul finished his beer, Juldeh brought him another one without being asked.

Abdul had greeted him almost genially and had chatted away, obviously enjoying himself. Jedi had said very little and was about to go upstairs when Abdul's tone abruptly changed to one of command.

"I have to take off my shoes; my feet are killing me," he said. "Mr. Thomas, take off my shoes for me."

Jedi could not believe that he had allowed himself to sink so low. This was the height of humiliation. He was also acutely aware of Juldeh eavesdropping from the kitchen, so he yelled,

"What! Do you think I am your servant? If you want to take off your shoes, take them off yourself."

"You are as good as my servant," Abdul retorted at the top of his voice. "I say take off my shoes!"

He leaned forward in his chair and stretched his feet towards Jedi. In apparent surrender, Jedi said, "Okay," but then called Juldeh from the kitchen and asked him to take off Abdul's shoes. He regretted it at once, realizing that by doing so he was conceding that Abdul had the right to give orders in his house. To make matters worse, Juldeh came and stood by the kitchen door, but gave his boss such a look of revulsion that Jedi wondered whether he would do as he was told. Abdul spared him the possibility of being humiliated by Juldeh by roaring,

"It is YOU I want to take off my shoes. If I wanted Juldeh, I would have asked him. Are you going to do it, or shall I do what I ought to do?" When Jedi still made no move, Abdul shouted with real menace in his voice,

"Do it now, Mr. Thomas."

"One day you will pay for this," Jedi murmured as he stooped to take of the shoes.

"We will see who will be doing the paying," Abdul remarked contemptuously.

Jedi felt close to tears, and dared not look at Juldeh. It was almost as though Abdul had promised Juldeh that he would do something in his boss's presence to show who was the master. Jedi flopped on to a chair and held his head in his hands. He was not crying, but the moans that came from him suggested that he was going through a terrible ordeal.

"Learn from me, Juldeh, how to make these high class people realize that we whom they despise can be their masters," Abdul said in the same contemptuous tone. "I have not finished with you yet, Mr. Thomas. Now, put the boots on again. I SAY, PUT THEM ON AGAIN!"

His voice was so loud that the walls of the house almost shook. Juldeh had already seen his boss humiliated, but he was shocked when he saw him rise silently and put Abdul's boots on again.

"Now kiss them," Abdul said.

What? Juldeh said to himself, *Is Mr. Thomas really going to kiss Abdul's shoes?* Yes, he was going to. He was actually doing it, although tears flowed freely down his face.

"Good," Abdul declared, rising to his feet. "I will now take my leave."

Allah Akbar! My boss is finished, Juldeh thought, shaking his head pityingly. *This is no longer a man.*

For a few weeks, nothing else happened. Abdul had made his point that he could come and go as he pleased and give orders whenever and to whomever he pleased, and no one would dare to thwart him. At times he arrived in the evenings when Jedi had returned home from work, but on these occasions the two men said very little to each other. He did not order Jedi around as he had done on that infamous occasion, merely sat in his favorite chair, helped himself to drinks from the fridge, and smoked contentedly. In any case, to avoid Abdul, Jedi started going out almost every evening. He sometimes visited relations, but mostly he went to bars and clubs and drank himself stupid. His deterioration therefore proceeded apace, and friends and acquaintances started observing that the once abstemious Jedi had taken seriously to drink.

Abdul started spending most days in Jedi's house, sleeping on the comfortable sofa, smoking, drinking Jedi's beer, and chatting with Juldeh with whom he was now on a footing of conviviality. Indeed, the less Juldeh respected Jedi, the more he was drawn towards Abdul who seemed to be a mine of information about what was really going on in the country: about the misdeeds of people in positions of power; about the immorality of those who considered themselves to be 'high class' like doctors, lawyers, professors, and other professionals; about the greed and dishonesty of the Lebanese and other businessmen close to the government. Because he frequented bars and clubs, and knew many taxi drivers, who were themselves mines of information, Abdul knew all the latest gossip. Juldeh, found it a pleasure to converse with someone as talkative as himself. Besides he was an ambitious young man who had not the slightest intention to remain a steward for long. He wanted to know what made the country tick, bide his time and, at the appropriate moment, make his move. This intimacy with Abdul was bringing him closer to that day.

One Saturday morning, as soon as Jedi let him in, Juldeh, who had become rather formal and restrained in his recent conversations with his boss, blurted out,

"Boss, have you heard the news?"

Jedi was taken aback, for it was a long time since Juldeh had been so ready to chat with him.

"What news?" he asked rather glumly.

"You know Pa Norman who lives at Wilberforce by the Regent Road junction!
He had this very beautiful daughter who got married to Lawyer Nicol. Well, she is dead."

"What!" Jedi shouted. "Do you mean that Omotunde Nicol is dead?"

"Yes, boss; she is dead."

Life expectancy in Sierra Leone was quite low and the string of obituary notices on the radio every day was usually very long indeed, so Jedi was used to reports of people, including well-known acquaintances, having died. But this one shocked him to the core. Omotunde Nicol was the beautiful younger sister of a fellow civil servant. Not only had she qualified as a banker, she had risen to a senior position in a leading bank, and had had the good fortune to marry an up-and-coming young lawyer. She also had two small children.

"What happened to her?" Jedi asked, still in shock. She could hardly have been more than thirty five.

"They say that her enemies threw 'allay' on her," Juldeh replied. "People who saw her before she died said her face looked as though it had been roasted."

Jedi thought of the beautiful face he remembered, and he shuddered.

"Poor girl," he said. "But she was such a good person: always friendly and smiling at everyone. What enemies could she have had?"

"This world is wicked, boss." Juldeh remarked like an old sage. "You never know who is your secret enemy. You cannot trust anyone. They say Lawyer Nicol is a handsome man and he has lots of money and that it was one of his many 'sweethearts' that did it. She wanted Mrs. Nicol out of the way so she could take her place in the house.

"Mrs. Nicol's mother is dead," Juldeh continued, "but they say that her father has gone almost crazy with grief. Mrs. Nicol was the only one who brought respectability to the family. The sons are useless."

"Poor woman," Jedi said again. "This world is so unfair! It seems as if it is the wicked who prosper."

A week later, Jedi went to the funeral. As is customary, he went first to the laying out at the Nicol home to file past the corpse and pay his respects. The body of the late Mrs. Omotunde Nicol was laid out in a magnificent mahogany casket lined with white lace and satin. Blue artificial flowers filled the inside of the lid. Omotunde Nicol herself was shrouded in an expensive light blue lace gown, with a coronet of blue flowers on her head, a bouquet of artificial flowers in her right hand, and a small Bible in her left. Only her face told the tragic story, for its features contrasted sharply with the exquisite blue shroud and the finely upholstered casket. She had a scowl on that once pretty face, a sure sign that she had died in agony, and though the mortician had done his best with powder and paint, one could still discern the ravages of the disease that killed her: the pock-marked black spots spreading thickly outwards from her nose and eyes. No wonder people had described her lovely olive skin as almost roasted. It did look roasted. What enemy, what evil monster could have done this? Jedi wondered in horror. What unsuspected rival could have so tortured such a promising young woman and cut her down in the prime of her life, depriving her family, especially her children, of her love and her nurturing goodness? The world, indeed, was wicked.

'Allay' is one of the triumphs of African science. There is nothing superstitious, or mysterious, or supernatural about it. Using 'allay' does not involve invoking spirits or other supernatural forces. It is practical, tangible, and entirely human, like poison or some other chemical weapon. There are various rumors about how the deadly stuff is produced, but only the members of certain secret societies know for certain. Because of its effects on the human skin, some people believe that crocodile skin is an important ingredient; others say that finely ground glass is another; others that fine sand forms part of it, as do pepper, the skin of chickens, and certain leaves. No outsider knows for sure. And there are various kinds of 'allay' with varying degrees of deadliness. Some only make its victims itch and scratch for the rest of their miserable lives. Others cause death after several years of itching and visitation by all kinds of rashes and skin diseases. The most deadly causes death in a few weeks or months and affects not only the skin, but also the blood and vital organs. There are antidotes for some kinds of 'allay', but for the deadliest, there is none.

Jedi had heard of one so deadly that the victim scratched continuously, no matter what treatment he was given, and eventually scratched his entire skin off, exposing the raw flesh beneath. He drove home from that heart-rending funeral pondering the wickedness of humanity. Man was indeed a beast, and the world was a jungle. There was that Abdul to prove it. Look at the way he had tortured him and reduced him to servitude and almost nothingness! Abdul had made him a shadow of his former self, someone whom friends and acquaintances now regarded with pity or scorn, depending on their disposition.

All at once, Jedi experienced a jolt so severe that his body jumped in the driver's seat as though he had been stung on his buttocks by a bee. He almost lost control of the car, and had to pull up by the kerb.

What had caused this tremendous jolt? It was the realization that in 'allay' he had the perfect weapon with which to get rid of that wicked, repulsive, sadistic, slime ball once and for all. Why had it not occurred to him before? Jedi wondered, feeling so elated that he cried out "Alleluia!" as he resumed his drive back to his home on Juba Hill. With 'allay', he would not be using any supernatural or mysterious agents whose effects were uncertain. He would be using one whose effectiveness had been scientifically proved. No duplicitous, double-speaking Pa Kelfala would be involved either. Besides, from what he had heard, one sent the 'allay' on to the victim in such a way that no one saw you do it; no one could link you with it. No western-trained forensic scientist would, as far as he knew, be able to trace the cause of death to you. It was impossible for the murderer to be discovered and the laws of Sierra Leone had made no provision for people who killed their opponents with 'allay.' Using it had all the anonymity and secrecy of Pa Kelfala's procedure without its uncertainties. It was just the thing. If he could only get hold of 'allay,' he would rid the world of that vermin, Abdul.

Jedi was whistling exuberantly as he entered his house that evening. He had not felt so happy in a long time. He took a bath, ate a heavy dinner, and drank a whole bottle of whisky before going to bed.

CHAPTER 12

Jedi spent the next few days working out the mechanics of procuring the 'allay.' In his position, and with his wide circle of friends and acquaintances, he had the contacts to be able to do it. That was one thing he had: contacts. There were lots of messengers and junior workers in his Ministry who would know of such things. He also knew several members of all sorts of secret societies. He knew them well enough to be able to say he wanted to procure 'allay' without having to tell them why he wanted it or for whom. He only needed to introduce the subject in a roundabout way and he was sure to get it. Once he had it, Abdul, the hog, was finished. This time he did not wonder about the morality of what he was planning, nor did he attempt to reconcile it with Christian principles. He simply assumed that the planned act was perfectly justified. Abdul was a venomous beast of prey, a pest, a parasite; he was little better than a terrorist. Such vermin needed to be cleared off the face of the earth and in getting rid of him, he would be doing the world a tremendous service.

Jedi's determination was reinforced when he went home after work one day and found Abdul comfortably relaxing, as he often did these days, on the sofa in the lounge and smoking a cigarette. There was a half empty bottle of beer on a stool by him. Jedi merely acknowledged his presence. He knew that when Abdul felt ready to do so, he would leave, perhaps without even saying goodbye. Soon after Jedi came home, Juldeh left for the day and Jedi went to have his dinner which, as usual, Juldeh had left on the table, in dishes wrapped in a blanket. The dining area was merely a raised continuation of the lounge, so Abdul could see him as he ate.

"By the way," Abdul called out to him from the lounge, "that your boy, Juldeh, can work wonders in the kitchen. Were you the one who taught him to cook like that? I almost licked my fingers after eating that okra stew. I am sure I ate too much. Look how high my stomach is."

Hog, Jedi thought sourly and did not respond aloud. *You want me to know that you have also been helping yourself to my food, and that Juldeh has been feeding you. Your death warrant has been signed. It will give me so much pleasure to see that face of yours in a coffin.*

He then thought of the irony involved when people pranced about dancing, eating, and enjoying themselves, not knowing that someone somewhere had already planned their deaths, and that within a few months, or weeks, or days, or hours or even minutes they would be dead. It was like the wealthy man in the Bible who said to himself that he would take his ease and eat and drink and be merry, not knowing that the Almighty had already decreed his death and was saying, "Thou fool! This night thy life shall be required of thee." Jedi felt a sudden surge of power as he thought this. Why? He would be like God himself. He had decreed the death of an unsuspecting victim who was at that very moment eating, drinking, and taking his ease. It was a great feeling to have absolute control over the life of another human being! Nothing could be better than that.

With thoughts like these going through his mind, Jedi could not have cared less whether Abdul left early or late. However, he was surprised when at ten thirty that night Abdul still showed no signs of leaving.

"Isn't it about time you went home?" Jedi asked indifferently.

"Oh," Abdul replied with equal nonchalance, "didn't Juldeh tell you? I am not going 'home' from now on; I shall be staying here. I brought my things over this morning, and Juldeh put them in the guest bedroom downstairs. That will be my room. I shall be staying here until further notice."

Jedi's entire body went completely rigid for a moment.

"How do you mean you will be staying here until further notice? I have not asked you to stay. You did not tell me you wanted to stay. I do not want you to stay; and this is my house, not yours. You cannot stay here."

But even as he protested, he knew he was powerless to stop Abdul. Experience so far had shown him that this young man would do whatever he wanted. Indeed, Abdul shouted,

"You are wrong, Mr. Thomas. This house is as good as mine. I own you. You belong to me. I can do whatever I want with you. I can surrender you up to the law and to trial, imprisonment and death, if I choose to. You are mine. And if you are mine, whatever you have is also mine. This is my house and I shall go and come as I please and stay in it for as long as I please. There is nothing you can do about it, and you had better not even try."

With that, Abdul went into the guest room. Jedi could hear him fidgeting about for a while. Then he emerged with what looked like a toilet bag in his hand, went into the bathroom and had a bath while whistling all the time, went back into the bedroom, slammed the door, and retired for the night.

Abdul's behavior would normally have aroused Jedi's anger, for his house was his most prized possession. The thought of someone else, particularly an enemy, trying to take it over would have brought him close to having a heart attack. On this occasion, however, he was able to react with equanimity because he was sure Abdul's days were numbered. Let him act as though he owned the house; he would be merely taking enough rope to hang himself. Abdul's move merely reinforced Jedi's determination to pursue his plan much more expeditiously. He made a mental note before he went to bed that night to skin Juldeh alive the next day for not mentioning that Abdul intended to stay in his house indefinitely. But then, what would be the point? Even though it was still he who paid Juldeh's wages at the end of the month, he knew he had almost completely lost Juldeh's loyalty and the authority he once had over him. If anything, it was Abdul who now seemed to command Juldeh's loyalty and even respect. *Never mind*, thought Jedi; *all that will change soon.*

It took him another three weeks to procure the 'allay.' For one thing, he had to make very careful and discreet inquiries. And for another, he wanted to make absolutely sure that he obtained the most deadly kind. He could not afford to take any more risks. When one went to a supplier and asked for that kind of 'allay', both the supplier and the customer knew that murder was involved, although both pretended that this was not the case. The supplier knew that, in a sense, he was being an accessory to a murder, although he pretended that he was doing no more than a pharmacist who sold rat poison. The difference, of course, was that in this case the venomous substance was definitely going to be used on a human being and its effect would almost certainly be fatal. The whole process had to be handled delicately. Besides, the 'allay' was rather expensive and, in his reduced circumstances, Jedi had to wait until he received his salary at the end of the month.

Jedi stared in awe and wonder when his supplier brought out the amazing powder and proceeded to put it into a flutelike container about nine inches long. It was made from the hollow stem of the paw-paw leaf and therefore known as a paw-paw gun. One end of it had been covered with a kind of transparent material as well as a cork to prevent the substance from leaking out. The supplier sealed the other end with the same material that would allow someone's breath to go right through it. He then provided further covers for both ends of the container. The idea was that the person administering the 'allay' should be able to blow it on to his victim without being seen. Even if the victim noticed him, he or she might not realize what was about to happen because the container looked like a child's toy or a strange kind of pipe. Jedi listened carefully to all the instructions, for he certainly did not intend to kill himself.

He was feeling on top of the world as he drove home that evening, with one of the most potent weapons in the world in his hands. That evening, and for the next few days until he decided on a suitable time to administer the substance, he could afford to put up with Abdul's insults. And during the three or four weeks since he moved into the house Abdul had behaved with the most intolerable arrogance, barking out orders to both Juldeh and Jedi. Jedi now complied with his numerous orders, reluctantly, but without questioning him. Abdul complained that Jedi gave Juldeh insufficient food to cook and ordered him to put out more. He was fed up with eating rice and would like to eat 'foofoo' and bitter leaf stew the next day. He had invited two friends to visit him, so Jedi had better make sure there would be enough food and drinks for three people. Hadn't Jedi realized that there was no longer any Heineken beer in the fridge? He had better make sure that there was Heineken beer tomorrow, or else... There had not been enough hot water when he had wanted to take his bath that morning; Jedi had better make sure the water heater was on all night so he could have enough hot water for his bath in the morning. And Jedi had better not stay up so late watching television or video because that disturbed him on those evenings when he wanted to go to sleep early. In fact, he would now decide when the television was to be switched off every night. Then, the main gate had to be left unlocked until he came in for the night, and he needed his own key to the front door because it was demeaning for him to knock on the door or ring the bell whenever he came home late. The commands went on and on and on, but Jedi put up with it all very patiently, because he knew that the end was near. He would watch Abdul lying drunk on the sofa, or swinging contentedly on the hammock on the balcony, and say to himself, *You fool! If you only knew what I have planned for you! If you only knew that in a few months or weeks you will be six feet under and that handsome form will be food for worms! If you only knew!*

Abdul was a nuisance in another way. Word soon spread through the ministry, the church and other branches of the grapevine, that Jedi harbored in his house a young man of very dubious character, who was eating him out of house and home. Some busybodies deliberately visited Jedi so that they could see this young man with their own eyes. They later reported that they had heard him giving orders both to Jedi and his servant. Imagine that! Giving orders to the Permanent Secretary, Jedidiah Thomas! Besides, this young man seemed to have very sloppy and unhygienic habits. In spite of Juldeh's efforts to clean up after him, he had almost succeeded in turning that elegant house into a pigsty. Who was this young man? What hold did he have on Jedi? All kinds of rumors circulated: that he might be an illegitimate son who, for one reason or another, Jedi did not wish to acknowledge publicly; that he was perhaps the leader of a gang of illicit diamond miners who worked for Jedi up country and brought him precious stones that he smuggled out of the country and sold for millions, then salted the funds in a Swiss bank account. Other rumors came pretty close to the truth, suggesting that the young man probably had information that, if known, would land Jedi in jail. Maybe he knew that Jedi had appropriated millions and millions of money from his ministry's account for his own use; many Permanent Secretaries had done it in the past. And so the rumors continued to fly. Jedi felt he could allow them to fly because the end was near.

It then occurred to him that Abdul's decision to come and live with him was a godsend. It would make it so much easier for him to catch Abdul in a perfect position to administer the 'allay.' It must have been God himself who had sent Abdul into his trap. Yes! The ways of God were inscrutable. God had made Abdul walk into the deadly trap with his own two feet. God was going to use Abdul's very avarice and arrogance to destroy him. To put it another way, God was going to let Abdul kill himself. Jedi began to see the hand of Providence in everything that was happening and felt even more justified in planning the murder. God himself was helping him get rid of one of the most venomous snakes on earth. He was merely being God's agent.

He had decided on the date on which he was going to administer the death dealing substance, but a few days before that day, Abdul dropped what, in other circumstances, would have been another devastating bombshell. Jedi had done his best to avoid him, to ensure that, if possible, they were not in the same room together. Whenever Abdul was eating in the dining area or was relaxing on the sofa in the lounge, Jedi went upstairs and stayed there. In fact, he was now spending most of his time in his bedroom.

On that day, Abdul swept into his bedroom, without knocking and without announcing himself. He did not give Jedi time to get over his surprise and disgust before saying,

"Mr. Thomas, I have been thinking that since you have agreed that I now virtually own this house, you should make a will and bequeath it to me." Jedi had already jumped out of bed when Abdul appeared so unceremoniously. He now shouted,

"What! You want me to alter my will and leave my house to you?"

Yes," Abdul replied as if he was making the most reasonable request. "Make a new will leaving the house to me."

Ever since Jedi decided to kill Abdul with 'allay' his timidity had lessened slightly, so he mustered enough spirit to say, "Oho! You want me to leave you my house in a will so that you can kill me and then take possession?"

"Mr. Thomas," Abdul said patiently, "Making a new will leaving me the house would merely be putting on paper what is already a fact. Okay! If you are afraid that a will might be forecasting your death, you can make a deed of gift and give me the house. In fact, a deed of gift is better. Then I won't have to wait until you are dead, and you needn't be afraid that I will try to kill you so as to get the house. The house would already be mine."

Jedi stared at Abdul, realizing now that all his moves had been tending towards this: absolute possession and mastery. This would be the culmination of his devilish plans. Had he not had a remedy for his tribulation concealed in his bedroom, Jedi would probably have fallen down and died on the spot; but he did have a remedy and the thought of it made him respond to Abdul's demand with remarkable composure.

"All right! I shall think about it and see what can be done."

"Just do it," Abdul snapped and left the room.

This latest demand convinced Jedi that he really had no choice but to put an end to Abdul's life. This bully was threatening to go to the police and report that he had committed a murder if he didn't give him his house. And Abdul had proved that he was perfectly capable of doing what he threatened to do. He had already reduced him to a nervous wreck and to slavish impotence. He had corrupted his houseboy. He had damaged his reputation and squandered almost all his assets. He had to be got rid of and fast.

Jedi decided to administer the 'allay' on the next Saturday night. Abdul usually came home drunk on Saturday nights after his debauchery at the 'Sunday Schools' and night-clubs. He always went to bed immediately, and fell into a drunken stupor. Jedi's plan was to go quietly into Abdul's room when he was in that state and administer the substance. On this Saturday, however, Abdul inexplicably came home earlier than usual. He was quite drunk, though, but instead of going to bed, he stripped off his shirt and his trousers, went upstairs to the balcony, and lay in the hammock. In spite of his drunkenness, he still ordered Jedi to bring him a beer but had hardly finished it when he fell deeply asleep. Again, Jedi realized that Abdul, or perhaps God himself, had presented him with the perfect opportunity. He did not now have to sneak into Abdul's bedroom downstairs. He could administer the substance right there, and at his leisure.

Jedi went to his bedroom for the paw-paw gun. To give himself extra protection, he covered himself well and put on a pair of gloves before handling the deadly contraption. He fondled it gently and lovingly, sliding his hand over its entire nine-inch length. This would be his deliverer. He then went out to the verandah and took up his position on a seat opposite Abdul. Since obtaining his 'remedy' he had begun to regard Abdul almost with indifference; but now, as he prepared to take his revenge, he was overwhelmed by feelings of disgust and hatred for this despicable thug. How could he have allowed himself to be defeated and enslaved by this vermin, this slime ball? Stripped of the fine clothes and gold chains he had bought with Jedi's money, Abdul looked what he really was: filth from Freetown's worst gutters. He was sweating profusely and his body was no longer attractive, for he had developed a potbelly that was already beginning to hang over his pants in folds. He really looked like an oversized hog as he lay there snoring. Jedi thought he had never heard such a disgusting snore. It was just like the sound from an enormous thirty-year-old car with a broken muffler and worn out plugs. By killing Abdul, he would be preventing some unfortunate woman from spending, perhaps the rest of her life, having to listen to such a disgusting noise. Abdul's jaw hung wide open as well, and because of his drunken orgy the breath coming from his mouth and nostrils was revolting. From time to time, he belched and broke wind unconsciously. *How could I, Jedidiah Thomas, with my education, status, and connections have allowed myself to be associated with a beast like this?* Jedi thought for the hundredth time.

He took up his paw-paw gun and prepared to administer death, again realizing his good fortune. The hand of God had not only brought Abdul home early and on to the verandah, it had also made him strip almost naked in preparation to receive the 'medicine.' Administered to someone who was fully clothed, the 'allay' would still have been effective, but it would be more deadly if it made direct contact with the skin. Besides, Abdul's sweat would spread it quickly over his whole body and diffuse it easily through his pores, helped by the way he kept rubbing himself in his sleep. The situation was perfect.

Jedi took up the paw-paw gun, removed the corks at either end, pointed the contraption towards Abdul, and blew, and blew and blew. He could see the tiny particles of the substance going towards the unconscious Abdul. Unlike the episode with Pa Kelfala's mirror, Jedi did not blow with any strong feeling, because his supplier had told him that to be really effective this substance had to be gently and deliberately blown. So Jedi blew gently, but he still rejoiced that he was blowing death to his enemy. Apart from the particles of powder, Jedi could also feel a kind of heat radiating from the paw-paw gun. This was supposed to be one of the characteristics of effective 'allay', so Jedi was sure that what he was doing would have the desired effect. He directed the paw-paw gun towards every inch of Abdul's body: his head and neck, chest, stomach, crutch, thighs, arms and legs, and toes. He even leaned forward slightly and directed some of it down his back. When he was satisfied that Abdul was covered in 'allay', he returned to his bedroom, concealed the paw-paw gun that he felt he ought to keep as a souvenir, and lifted up his hands to give God glory and thanksgiving.

Two hours later, Abdul was still soundly asleep on the hammock, so Jedi roused him saying it was time he went downstairs to his own bedroom, so the door connecting the balcony with the rest of the house could be padlocked for security. Still groggy, Abdul obeyed like a lamb. *Things are already beginning to change,* Jedi thought.

The next day was Sunday, and Jedi went to church. As usual when things were going well for him, he praised his maker with wholehearted exuberance. His friends and acquaintances concluded that his situation must be improving. They congratulated him on how much better he was looking and wished him well. Jedi did not return home till about three in the afternoon because he was indulging in the usual Sunday revelry with his fellow sidesmen. He arrived at Juba Hill in jubilant mood to discover that Abdul had only just got up. Although he had slept for about seventeen continuous hours, he still looked bleary-eyed, his face puffy. Suddenly, he gave himself two tremendous smacks: one on his cheek and one on his thigh.

"These damned mosquitoes!" he exclaimed. "Mr. Thomas, can't you buy some Shelltox and spray the house regularly? It seems to be full of mosquitoes. They have been biting me since I got out of bed and, what is worse, they are so clever: I can't even see them." With that he gave himself another smack.

Later that evening, Jedi noticed that Abdul hardly sat in one place for long. He seemed extremely uncomfortable and constantly scratched and smacked himself. He wore only shorts, so Jedi saw that welts and blisters were beginning to form on his face, arms, and legs. He stormed out to the verandah where Jedi was sitting and shouted,

"Spray this house now! I can't stand these mosquitoes any more. Perhaps you want them to drive me away, but I tell you, nothing will drive me out of this house. It is mine."

"You know that this is Sunday and all the shops are shut," Jedi said. "I will buy some mosquito spray tomorrow. In the meantime, the best thing for you to do is to drink some whisky and go to sleep. That will help you not to feel the mosquito bites. And with a lot of whisky in your blood, the mosquitoes will not like the taste and stop biting you. They will think that the whisky will make them drunk."

The last statement was intended as a joke, but Abdul apparently believed it for he said, "That is true," and went and drank several glasses of whisky. He retired early, but Jedi could still hear loud groaning, smacking, and swearing, and knew that Abdul was beginning to suffer horribly. Jedi smiled triumphantly as he remembered one of his favorite lines from Shakespeare: "Work on, my medicine, work."

The next morning Jedi let Juldeh in as usual, and started to get himself ready to go to the office. He was startled when Juldeh rushed upstairs, crying out,

"Boss, come down quickly. Mr. Abdul seems to be very ill. I think he is going crazy."

Jedi went downstairs to find Abdul shouting at the top of his lungs and scratching desperately and rubbing himself against any suitable surface, like a molting snake rubbing itself against rocks to remove its old skin.

"See what your mosquitoes have done to me?" he screamed.

"But this has nothing to do with mosquitoes," Jedi said, feigning concern as he pointed at the welts and rashes and sores that were rapidly forming all over Abdul's body. "It looks like 'fresh blood' to me."

"They say lime-juice mixed with ashes is very good for fresh blood," Juldeh advised. "I have some lime and ashes. Let me bring some."

"Go and get them!" Abdul roared. "Can't you see I am suffering? My whole body is burning like hell."

Juldeh soon brought the mixture of lime-juice and ashes and, using a piece of cloth, started to rub it all over Abdul's body. Abdul screamed as the mixture was applied, and kept on screaming long after Juldeh had finished the application. He rolled off his bed on to the ground, shouting wildly. Far from improving the situation, the mixture of lime-juice and ashes had, if anything, made matters worse. Outwardly, Jedi still appeared to be concerned, but inwardly he was in high glee. Things were going even better than he had expected. It had been only a matter of hours rather than days or weeks before the stuff began to work. The supplier must have given him the most effective kind.

After a while, Jedi ignored the commotion in the guest room and went to have breakfast in preparation for leaving the house. Abdul stormed into the dining area, panting as he rubbed himself hard all over.

"This thing is getting worse. I can't stand it! I can't bear it!" He was actually crying now. "No human being was meant to suffer like this. I tell you, I am in hell. Look at my face! It is like something that has just started to roast. You will have to take me to the hospital right now."

"My, friend," Jedi said, "I would have loved to help, but I am already late for work and I have an important meeting with the Minister this morning. I tell you what," he added, as though trying to accommodate Abdul. "As soon as the meeting is over I will rush over here and take you to the hospital."

With that, Jedi left for work, thinking, *Who is going to take that one to the hospital? Let him suffer. He has made me suffer, so, why should he not suffer now?*

At work that day Jedi was at the peak of his form and his staff and colleagues recognized the change in him. He had lied when he told Abdul that he had an early meeting with the Minister, but he did have one later in the morning with other senior officials who were pleasantly surprised at the return of his usual efficiency. He had mastered all the details of the matter to be discussed and was brimful of ideas as he steered the meeting on to a highly successful conclusion. Mrs. Cole and the other clerks and secretaries laughed uproariously at his jokes that day, and they rejoiced that he was on top form once more. Their office had returned to something like normalcy.

When Jedi returned home that evening and asked for Abdul, Juldeh breathed a heavy sigh,

"Boss, he is no longer here. When we did not see you, I got him a taxi to take him to the hospital. If I had not seen it with my own two eyes I would not have believed what happened. That Mr. Abdul who seemed so powerful was crying like a baby. He was begging God to come and help him and he never stopped scratching and rolling on the ground or on his bed. The swellings on his body and his face had increased, and they were turning black. Even the neighbors heard his screams and started looking out of their windows to see what was happening. There are bloodstains all over his bed. Boss, mortal man is nothing !"

Jedi listened without showing any emotion, then quietly asked Juldeh to strip Abdul's bed and burn the bedclothes, after which he was to collect all Abdul's belongings and put them in a suitcase ready to be disposed of. He did not tell

Juldeh that, but he knew that Abdul would not be returning to his house.

Later that evening, Jedi drove to the hospital to see for himself how much Abdul had deteriorated. He went first to the outpatients department to inquire as discreetly as possible about a young man who was brought in that morning with some kind of skin disease. However, he did not have to, because that was just what the nurses and orderlies were discussing animatedly. He merely had to look as if he was waiting for someone and listen to their conversation.

"I am sure there is no hope for him," said one of the nurses who had obviously witnessed Abdul's arrival at the hospital. "You should see the sores and blisters all over his body! And the swellings are as black as though he was burnt by fire in those places. His face is almost twice its size...He was squealing like a hog whose throat is about to be cut, cursing God and everything else he could think of."

"They say his body has already begun to stink," another one said. "Such a young man! It is really terrible."

"I am sure it is 'allay'," said the first nurse. "I have seen several cases like that." Then one of the orderlies wanted to know where the young man had been taken.

"To ward five," put in another nurse, "but since he did not come with any money or with people to find a doctor for him, no one has touched him. He has not even been given a bed yet. They have just left him on the floor in the corridor outside the ward. The other patients have started to complain that he is disturbing them with his screaming. This world is a *bad* place," she added, compressing her lips to emphasize the point. "That is why one should fear God and always do what is right."

Jedi was superbly pleased with what he had heard. But to make absolutely sure he went up to Ward Five and peeped into the corridor, trying to make sure that no one noticed him.

It was not difficult to ascertain where Abdul was lying on the floor. The fearful howls proclaimed his presence as well as the horrible stench emanating from his body. There was a real possibility that he might start rotting above ground. His face was almost unrecognizable; it was so swollen. Wrapped in a grayish bloodstained sheet that must once have been white, he already looked like a corpse.

Jedi was perfectly satisfied. Things could not have gone better. He drove home and slept the sleep of the just. The next day and for a few days afterwards he avoided discussing Abdul with Juldeh. He was aware of the growing respect his steward had developed for the thug, and thought Juldeh must be one of the few people who would be concerned about Abdul. As far as he, Jedi, was concerned, he could not care less. In fact, Abdul's demise could not happen soon enough for him.

Juldeh must himself have realized that his master would be far from sympathetic towards Abdul because he did not raise the subject. When his master ordered him to burn the bedclothes in Abdul's room and to collect his belongings and pack them in a suitcase, he realized that Jedi was already excising Abdul out of his life and his house and would not welcome any conversation about him. Juldeh went to the hospital to visit Abdul once after work, and he was horrified by what he saw. Not even Abdul's blistered and blood-soaked condition when he left the Juba Hill house could have prepared him for this. He found Abdul on the floor and almost naked because his rolling about and frantic scratching had exposed most of his body, which was now swollen to twice its size and covered all over with blisters, swellings and black spots. Not only blood, but pus and other slimy substances were oozing from the wounds, causing an unbearable stench. In unimaginable agony, Abdul only stopped screaming to catch his breath, calling on everyone and anyone to pour ice-water or ice-cubes over him because his entire body was burning up.

Sometimes he called on God to have mercy on him; at other times he cursed God, his mother, and all his ancestors for bringing him into the world to undergo such suffering. He did not seem to recognize Juldeh, merely staring at him blankly for a moment before another bout of screaming.

Juldeh could not stand the sight for more than fifteen minutes or so and fled from the hospital exclaiming that if there was a hell, it was right here on earth. Juldeh never returned to the hospital, but Jedi did, about a week after Abdul was first admitted. He wanted to witness Abdul's suffering and find out how far his body had disintegrated. Moreover, seeing Abdul in that sorry state would confirm the fact that he had regained his power and was master of his destiny once more.

However, when he walked up the stairs to Ward 5, there was no Abdul to be seen on the floor in the corridor. Even though he did not want people to know that there had been any connection between the miserable patient and himself, Jedi simply had to find out what had happened to Abdul, so he went up to the nurse in charge of the ward and asked for the young man who had been lying out in the corridor.

"Oh," said the nurse, "he died last night; the body is in the mortuary. Are you related to him? Or are you from Juba Hill?"

Jedi felt a surge of anger and disgust that anyone should imagine him remotely related to that bundle of stinking flesh.

"Oh, no! No, no." he answered almost shuddering. "I only met him briefly once through my steward. It was my steward who asked me to do him the favor of looking in on the young man when he knew I was coming to visit someone else. I shall now have the sad task of telling him that his friend is dead."

"We need someone to identify the body and claim it for burial," the nurse went on. "No one has come forward so far and he never gave us the name of any relations, just an address at Juba Hill. Can you identify him?"

Jedi was loath to admit that he even knew Abdul, but he was anxious to see for himself that his enemy was truly dead, so he agreed to identify the body, though he insisted that that was all he was willing to do.

The mortuary was cold enough, but in a terrible state of disorganization, with corpses lying all over the place, exposed on concrete slabs. Jedi wondered what happened when one of the frequent power outages occurred, and shuddered inwardly. He was visibly shaken when the mortuary attendant led him to a slab occupied by a shrouded corpse that seemed to be much bulkier than any of the others.

"This is it," he said.

What a horrible transformation had occurred in Abdul! Jedi almost retched at the sight and smell of the corpse and wished that he had not come after all. The orderly went on,

"Someone will have to come and claim the body soon, or it will have to go to a pauper's grave. We really cannot keep it here much longer."

As Juldeh had done before him, Jedi fled. However, as he raced home in his car, the feeling of nausea that had almost overwhelmed him when he saw Abdul's body disappeared and was replaced by a feeling of triumph and tremendous satisfaction. Yes! He had done it this time. He had finally got rid of his most deadly enemy. Abdul might have reduced him to a nervous wreck at one time, but he had succeeded in reducing him to a swollen, stinking corpse. This was mastery! This was power!

"Abdul!" he exulted. "Who is master now, enh? Who is master now? Alleluia!"

He rushed upstairs to his bedroom when he arrived, fell on his knees, and sang the whole of the "Te Deum" from memory.

The next day, Jedi casually informed Juldeh that Abdul had died at the hospital two days earlier. Juldeh said nothing, but Jedi could see that he was moved. *Isn't it strange*, Jedi thought, *how the most villainous people can sometimes inspire sympathy and loyalty. Juldeh will probably be the only person who will mourn for Abdul.* Neither of them mentioned Abdul for the rest of the day.

The next morning, Juldeh looked both bewildered and miserable when he came to work. In a voice full of pain, he said to Jedi,

"Boss, after I left you yesterday I went to the mortuary to see whether I could see Mr. Abdul's body because I knew I would probably not know when the funeral was going to be held. I wanted to take a last look at him." He paused to wipe a tear before going on. "Boss, they told me that they had already buried him. They said that no one came to claim the body and that it was swelling more and more every minute and already starting to rot. They said that the authorities at the Ministry of Health ordered immediate burial and they just put him on a stretcher and took him to Kingtom Cemetery in an old van. Mr. Abdul was buried like a pauper."

Just what he deserved, Jedi thought, not even trying to feign interest. *He died like a dog and was buried like a dog.* Since he made no comment, Juldeh carried on with his work, but later in the day asked what he should do with Abdul's belongings in the suitcase.

"Do anything you like," Jedi replied carelessly. "You can even keep them for yourself."

"Free at last!" he shouted as he prepared for bed that night, congratulating himself on the skill and efficiency with which he had dispatched his deadly enemy and rid himself of the terrible burden on his shoulders. What was even more satisfying was that, with the possible exception of Pa Kelfala, he had solved his problem without discussing it with anyone.

From now on he could get on with his life in peace. There were still the two police constables, Demoh and Bayoh, but they could do absolutely nothing without Abdul. They did not even know the real nature of his crime. The stupid fools seemed to think that it had been some kind of illicit sexual liaison between himself and Abdul, which was why they were blackmailing him. They would know that without Abdul they would be in no position to press any charges, so, presto! The threat from that quarter, too, was over. Alleluia! He had already regained most of his reputation and social acceptability, and conditions in his office had returned to normal. He was already performing his various official duties with his usual thoroughness and skill and the same applied to his religious duties at the church. Civil servants of his rank had recently been given a massive pay rise and he had started saving money again, so he was sure he would soon rebuild his financial fortunes. His haggard appearance at the height of Abdul's power over him had already begun to disappear, and it was just a matter of time before he regained his good looks. Yes! God had helped him take care of his problems. And once again, life was good. Wasn't God great! Alleluia!

His euphoria lasted until the next day when he walked into his lounge after work and saw not only Constables Bayoh and Demoh relaxing in his luxurious chairs, but also his steward Juldeh. Jedi's initial astonishment changed to anger at the sight of the two corrupt policemen. Feeling he could afford to be haughty with them now that their main instrument of blackmail was dead, he demanded of Juldeh,

"What are these two men doing in my lounge? Why did you let them in?"

Instead of jumping to attention to answer his master, Juldeh continued to sit there, as though *he* now owned the place, looking at him calmly and with the utmost disdain. It was Constable Bayoh who spoke first.

"Mr. Thomas," he said, "before you start behaving like God Almighty, we shall get straight to the point. You remember Abdul, the young man who came to us with a report about you and threatened to expose you and accuse you of serious crimes. Well, your steward here firmly believes you may have had a hand in his recent death from a strange skin disease. But we will go into that later. What we are here for is to investigate the death of a young girl. You knew her: Emma King. She disappeared some time ago."

Thinking his heart would stop, Jedi sank into the nearest chair. Just when he thought that the threat of exposure and punishment for Emma's death had been permanently removed, it had reared its head again, and this time the police seemed to know exactly what had happened. Somehow they had got to know about his connection with her death. Surely, this could not be happening! In reply to Constable Bayoh's question he spluttered,

"Em... Emma...Emma...? .I...I can't recall anyone by that name."

"Can't you, Mr. Thomas?" Constable Bayoh inquired blandly, "You can't remember the schoolgirl you were having an affair with and who disappeared without trace? Well, let us refresh your memory. Abdul Sanusi was this girl's boyfriend, as you very well know. After her disappearance, he came to live in your house and had been blackmailing you because he knew your secret. We knew that he was blackmailing you, but we did not know the exact nature of your secret crime. Anyway, Abdul felt that his life might be in danger, so he wrote everything down and put the document in a sealed envelope, and addressed it to me. He gave it to your steward with instructions to hand it to me if, and only if, anything were to happen to him. The document gives details of your relationship with Emma King and of her death and disappearance. Abdul claims that he was present on the fateful night and saw you carry the girl's body away in your car. He also witnessed your attempt to burn and bury her clothes and shoes. He claims that he saved the shoes which did not burn properly and kept them in this bag. Juldeh let me have it."

Juldeh handed over a white plastic bag from which Constable Bayoh pulled out a pair of half burnt black shoes. Jedi immediately recognized them as Emma's.

His whole body seemed to wilt and the confidence he had regained during the weeks following Abdul's death suddenly left him and he now looked and behaved like a guilty man. He could have denied everything that Constable Bayoh said Abdul had written. He could have told him that he did not try to burn any clothes, and that those shoes were not retrieved from his yard; that it was probably Abdul himself who killed the girl out of jealousy and was now trying to pin the blame on him. Abdul could not return from the grave to refute his own account. Without him and a body, the police would find it difficult to make a case. But Jedi was incapable of such clear thinking at that moment. Confronted for the first time with real evidence of a crime he knew or thought he had committed, he found himself assailed by a barrage of emotions. He started moaning deep in his throat like a dying man.

"Of course," Constable Demoh put in, "it won't be too difficult to prove that these were Emma's shoes and that they came from your compound where you had attempted to burn them. And also, juries tend to believe messages meant to be read after the death of their authors. After all, a man has no reason to lie from beyond the grave. The question now is, where is Emma's body?"

"Where is Emma's body, Mr. Thomas?" Constable Bayoh demanded, while Juldeh regarded his quailing boss with revulsion mingled with contempt.

"I do ..do...I do not know," Jedi replied in a feeble voice.

"Well," said Constable Demoh, "We'll find out in time. There are ways to make you talk."

All of a sudden, he changed his tone and sounded almost sympathetic as he continued to address the moaning and cowering Jedi.

"You must not consider that all is lost, Mr. Thomas. Of course, now that we are dealing with a case of murder, you will have to go to the police station and make a statement, and there will have to be an arrest and a trial. But in these matters there is always room for negotiation. Even judges and juries and our superintendent can be accommodating. Not all of us are unfeeling monsters. You can avoid the death penalty but of course, several other people will now have to be considered, including your steward, Juldeh, who came forward with Abdul's letter. You have your house which you can sell. Or to simplify matters you can just make a deed of gift in favor of Constable Bayoh, Juldeh, and myself. We will then see what we can do. Think about it, Mr. Thomas. We will leave you now, but we will be back at eight tomorrow morning to invite you to go with us to the Central Police Station. Don't even think of trying to leave town. You won't be able to escape."

All three then rose and left. Jedi remained sitting in the chair for about two hours, plunged in the deepest gloom. The game was up, it seemed. When the secret remained just between himself and Abdul, he believed that as long as he had money and other assets, he had the means to placate Abdul. But now Abdul was dead and the secret was out and he was in the hands of the police. They had not arrested him yet, but it was only a matter of time. And Juldeh, had turned against him. He had known that Juldeh was on friendly terms with Abdul, but would never have believed that his own steward would be the means of betraying him to the police. One could never trust anyone in this world. And now, it seemed that Juldeh also wanted to get in on the action. Hadn't Constable Demoh suggested that he would have to bribe other people? That included Juldeh. And, hadn't Constable Demoh implied that he could make his house over, to the three of them by a deed of gift? Was he suggesting that if he cooperated there might be no charges, or the charges would be less serious, or that the penalty would be reduced? Jedi was in too great a state of shock to think all this through clearly. All he knew was that he had neither the energy nor the will or the financial resources to endure blackmail all over again. Nor could he bring himself to face the terrible shame and disgrace of arrest, trial, imprisonment and possibly even hanging.

Some criminologists assert that it has been largely through giving in to a temptation to revisit the scene of the crime that some criminals have been caught. This may or may not be generally true. It was, however, certainly true in the case of Jedidiah Thomas. He finally emerged from his shocked stupor at about half past six that evening, rushed straight into his car and headed for the spot along the Peninsula road where he had parked it during that terrible storm more than a year ago. Why? Was he going to see whether the body was still there and whether the police might therefore be able to find it, or did he intend, somehow, to purge himself of his guilt by confronting his crime? Whatever his motives, he proceeded unerringly to the spot, left his car along the road, entered the bush, and headed for the gully. He looked forty feet down the gully and saw Emma's skeleton suspended on a long thick creeper. The whitish gray skull and other bones filled him with such horror and revulsion that he retched repeatedly. Could this be all that remained of that beautiful girl who had once aroused such intense desire in him and given him so much pleasure? Could he have ever been remotely connected with this…this thing? *What is man after all? Nothing,* he thought. Even if it had been his intention to retrieve Emma's remains for more thorough concealment, or to dispose of the skeleton somehow, the gully was much too deep for him to have done so. He turned abruptly, rushed back to his car as fast as the undergrowth would let him, and headed for home.

It was Juldeh and Constables Bayoh and Demoh who found him the next morning. Having decided that he could no longer work for someone for whom he felt the deepest scorn and revulsion and also that he could make money out of Jedi without being in his employ, Juldeh came to the house with the two constables to continue the dialogue of the previous evening and take whatever steps were necessary. At first, when Jedi did not come to open the gate which had been padlocked for the night, they thought that he must have absconded. However, they ruled that out when, having scaled the wall, Juldeh discovered Jedi's car still in the garage. They rang the doorbell, but there was still no response, so Juldeh scaled the balcony and peered into Jedi's bedroom through the window and curtains. He made out Jedi's entire six foot frame lying stretched out on his bed, completely motionless. When the police broke in, they discovered Jedi's body stone cold with a strange expression of serenity, even relief, on his face. The eyes stared calmly at the ceiling. Juldeh was moved by the sight of his employer lying there dead even though he had judged him so harshly during the last few weeks. He performed one last service for Jedi by closing his eyes forever.

The coroner's verdict was that Jedi died of a massive heart attack during the night, not knowing that Jedi's death was really suicide while the balance of his mind was disturbed, as they say. How could he have known that Jedi was in such a state of depression, bewilderment, shock, and despair, and that he had felt such a sense of entrapment that he decided he had only one way out: taking his own life. How could he have known that Jedi had thought about such a possibility at the lowest point in his enforced dealings with Abdul and had acquired a large quantity of a deadly angina-inducing drug just in case life became unendurable. He had swallowed the entire contents of the packet as soon as he returned home. A more thorough autopsy would have uncovered the poisoning, but one look at the huge blood clot in Jedi's heart had been enough for the pathologist.

Freetown was stunned by the untimely death of a man who seemed to be at the height of his powers, who seemed to have such a great future ahead of him, and who could reasonably have looked forward to another thirty years or so of productive life. In death, Jedi became something of a hero; only Constable Bayoh, Constable Demoh and Juldeh knew differently, but they kept the knowledge to themselves. The two constables were angry because they felt cheated of an income, and possibly even a house, that might have kept them comfortable for the rest of their lives. Juldeh, on the other hand, felt afraid. He was a devout Muslim, and saw the hand of God in all that had happened: Abdul had been a blackmailer and had died a horrible death; Mr. Thomas had committed murder and had died suddenly of a heart attack, possibly brought on by the fear of discovery; he, Juldeh, had befriended the blackmailer and had engaged in a sordid conspiracy against his employer. He had been sorely disappointed in his expectations and had even lost his job. Indeed, Allah was to be feared. Juldeh disappeared from public view and fled for safety to his native Guinea.

Jedi's funeral, a week later, was the biggest one Freetown had seen that year, with vigils held first at his church and another which lasted the rest of the night, at his home on Juba Hill. There were tributes galore at the church vigil. Jedi was praised to the skies as a man of unimpeachable integrity in these days when corruption was so rife, and as a brilliant civil servant of extraordinary efficiency and devotion to duty. Several tributes also recounted his unequalled service to his church and to his old school. He had, indeed, given selfless service to both church and state and was a model citizen in whose steps, it was hoped, young people would follow. His death was a sad loss to the entire country, another tribute declared.

The next day, Jedi's body was laid out in his church: a singular honor reserved only for the great and the good. The family had bought the best casket on the market and dressed him in his grey morning coat, formal striped trousers, winged collar, and a matching gray tie. He also had on the appropriate regalia of his Masonic lodge and his old school tie was folded and put beside his body. It was reported that thousands filed past the body and that for the funeral service itself, not only was the church packed to its full capacity, there were hundreds of people outside. In attendance were the church choir; all the church organizations; Jedi's Masonic lodge, dressed in their appropriate regalia; past students of Jedi's old High School; many members of the Young Men's Christian Association; lots of lay readers; and clergymen, even from other denominations. Appropriately, the opening hymn was one of Jedi's favorites: 'Alleluia! The strife is o'er, the battle done.' Led by two marching bands, the procession to the cemetery was hundreds of yards long and blocked traffic for hours to the delight of pedestrians and other onlookers, but to the great annoyance of motorists trying to get home after a hard day at the office. To await a joyful resurrection, Jedidiah Thomas was buried in a magnificent concrete vault with walls tiled in pale blue, and concrete slab covers so heavy that no grave-robber would ever be able to open it. As the ceremony ended, a trumpeter from the marching band of his old school played 'The last post' without a single false note.

Everyone agreed that it had been a fitting funeral and burial for such a pillar of the community.